MACMILLAN READERS
UPPER LEVEL

HERMAN MELVILLE

Moby Dick

Retold by John Escott

MACMILLAN

MACMILLAN READERS
UPPER LEVEL

Founding Editor: John Milne

The Macmillan Readers provide a choice of enjoyable reading materials for learners of English. The series is published at six levels – Starter, Beginner, Elementary, Pre-intermediate, Intermediate and Upper.

Level Control
Information, structure and vocabulary are controlled to suit the students' ability at each level.

The number of words at each level:

Starter	about 300 basic words
Beginner	about 600 basic words
Elementary	about 1100 basic words
Pre-intermediate	about 1400 basic words
Intermediate	about 1600 basic words
Upper	about 2200 basic words

Vocabulary
Some difficult words and phrases in this book are important for understanding the story. Some of these words are explained in the story, some are shown in the pictures, and others are marked with a number like this: ...^{3}. Words with a number are explained in the Glossary at the end of the book.

Answer Keys
An Answer Key for the *Points for Understanding* section and help with answers for the *Further Study Questions* can be found at www.macmillanenglish.com/readers

Contents

	A Note About The Author	4
	A Note About This Story	5
1	The Man Who Sold Heads	7
2	The Pequod	12
3	Elijah's warning	18
4	Captain Ahab	21
5	The Five "Ghosts"	26
6	"Lower the Boats!"	30
7	"Man Overboard!"	35
8	The Jungfrau	39
9	The Rose-bud	46
10	The Samuel Enderby	52
11	Queequeg's Coffin	56
12	Ahab's Dream	61
13	The Typhoon	66
14	The Rachel	70
15	Moby Dick!	78
16	Fedellah is Lost	85
17	The Second Hearse	89
	Points for Understanding	97
	Glossary	102
	Further Study Questions	107

A Note About The Author

The American writer, Herman Melville, was born in New York in 1819. He was one of eight children. Herman's father died when he was twelve years old, and a year later he left school and began working in a bank to help support his family. This was followed by jobs as a teacher and a newspaper reporter. Then, at the age of nineteen, he sailed on a merchant ship[1] to Liverpool in England. This was the first of several sea voyages[2] until, at the age of twenty-one, he joined the crew[3] of the whaling ship *Acushnet*.

Melville and another sailor left the *Acushnet* eighteen months after sailing from New York to travel around South America and across the Pacific Ocean. The two young men landed at the Marquesas Islands in the South Seas where they lived for a short time among cannibals[4]. Melville used this experience in his first book, *Typee: A Peep at Polynesian Life*, which was published in 1846. Two more books, *Omoo* (1847) and *Mardi and a Voyage Thither*, (1849) were also based on his South Seas adventures.

By 1850, Melville was married and he and his wife went to live in Pittsfield, Massachusetts in the eastern U.S.A. Here they became good friends and neighbors of Nathaniel Hawthorne, who was one of America's most famous writers. Melville greatly admired Hawthorne's work and was inspired and encouraged to write *Moby Dick* soon after the two men met. Melville dedicated the book to his friend when it was published in 1851.

However, Melville was disappointed when the book was not popular with readers or critics, and after this he wrote mostly short stories and poetry until his death in 1891.

It wasn't until the 1920s that some of Melville's unfinished manuscripts[5] were found by chance. At this point, the critics' interest in Melville's writing began to grow and *Moby Dick* finally became recognized as a classic American novel. It is now considered to be one of the greatest novels of all time.

A Note About This Story

Sperm whaling was an important American industry in the 1800s. Sperm oil was one of the main sources of fuel[6] until the discovery of petroleum in 1859. But whaling was also a dangerous business and newspapers often told stories of whaling ships that had been attacked or sunk whilst at sea. One of the most famous of these was the whaling ship, the *Essex*. This ship left Nantucket in 1819 to hunt whales in the South Pacific, and was expected to be away for two-and-a-half years. But on November 20, 1819, the *Essex* was struck by a huge sperm whale and it sank 3,700 km off South America. The crew were left afloat in small whaleboats for many months and most of them died from lack of food and fresh water.

Herman Melville would have read about the sinking of the *Essex* in one or more of the many newspaper reports and books that he studied about ships and whaling. He would also have known about the famous sperm whale, Mocha Dick, that lived close the island of Mocha, off southern Chile, in the Pacific Ocean.

Mocha Dick was a white whale who survived many battles with harpooners[7]. He was very fierce[8] when attacked and he drowned several whaleboat crews before he was finally killed. Dick was the name of the sailor who first hunted him.

Moby Dick is an adventure story and an account of whaling in the 1800s. But it is also as the story of an individual's struggle against fate or against nature, and about the battle between good and evil, the great white whale symbolizing evil. However, Ahab's determination to destroy the whale can be seen as evil and wicked too. *Moby Dick* is a book that can be read on many levels, and is a story that has entertained readers for more than a hundred years. No doubt it will continue to do so.

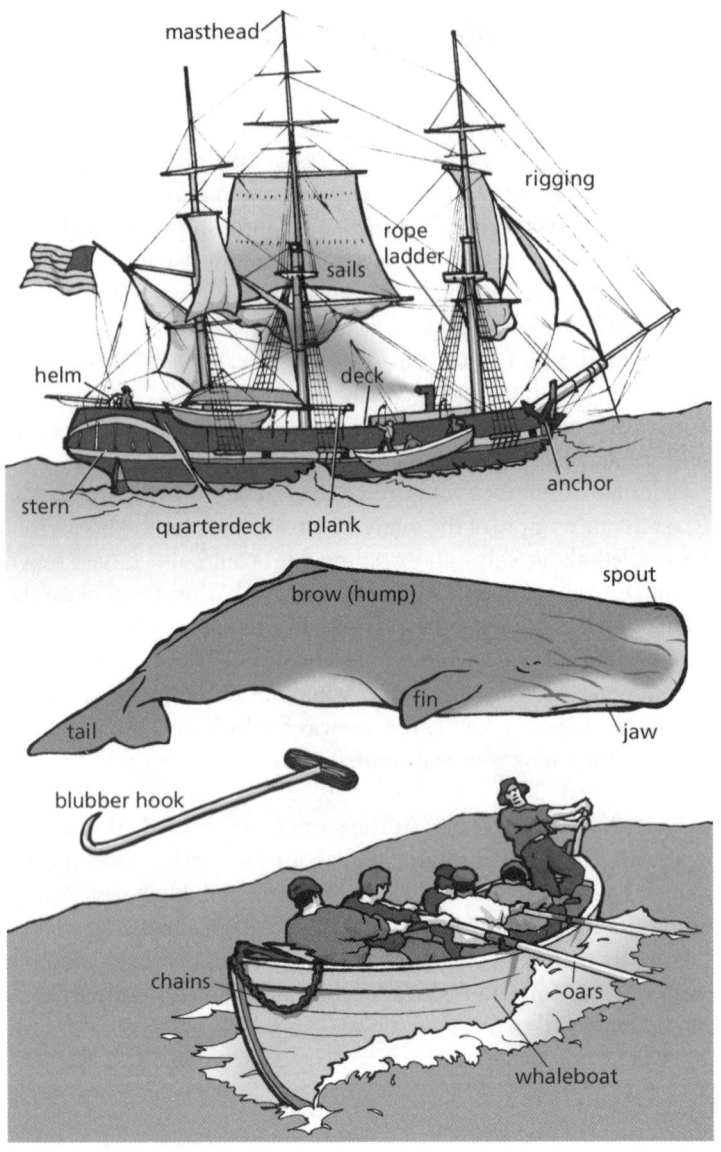

1
The Man Who Sold Heads

Call me Ishmael.
Some years ago, on a wet and miserable November day, I decided to get on a ship and sail to different parts of the world. There was nothing to interest me on shore and I was feeling irritable[9] and bad-tempered. Whenever I feel like this, I know that it is time for me to go to sea again. Not as a passenger though. For that you need money, and I never have enough. Nor as a ship's captain, for I do not want to be responsible for other men. It is as much as I can do to be responsible for myself. When I go to sea, I go as an ordinary sailor.

So I packed my old bag and left Manhattan to go to New Bedford, where I would get a boat to the island of Nantucket. Why Nantucket? Because this time I was going to look for work on a whaling ship! It was my dream to hunt and catch a whale, that magnificent[10] and mysterious creature of the sea. And all the biggest and best whaling ships sailed out of Nantucket Island, off the coast of Massachusetts.

I arrived in New Bedford on a Saturday night in December. I went straight to the docks but was disappointed to discover that the little boat for Nantucket had already sailed. There would not be another boat to the island until Monday.

I had very little money with me, for I had hoped to find a ship quickly. Now I had to find somewhere to eat and sleep, so I began to walk through the streets. Snow covered the ground and the ice-cold wind blew into my face. I passed several inns but they looked too expensive, so I went back down to the docks again. Here, in these dark and nearly empty streets, were the cheapest places to get a bed for the night.

The Man Who Sold Heads

After a time, a sign appeared over my head in the darkness. It hung outside an old wooden building.

The Spouter Inn—Landlord, Peter Coffin[11]

The place looked suitable, so I pushed open the door and went inside. I stepped into a long, badly lit room with blackened walls. There were harpoons and spears fixed to the walls, and a large painting of a whale and whaling ships.

I found Peter Coffin, the landlord, and explained that I needed a room for two nights.

"Every room and every bed is occupied," Coffin told me. "But you could share a bed with a harpooner. Are you going whaling?"

"Yes, I am," I answered.

"Then you'd better get used to sharing a bed," he said.

"All right," I replied. I was tired, and it was too cold and dark to walk the streets in a strange town to look for another place to stay.

Soon after, the landlord brought me a supper of meat and potatoes and boiling hot tea. It was very good.

"Where's the harpooner who will share my bed?" I asked him when I had finished eating.

"He'll be here soon," said Coffin. "He's late tonight, but perhaps he can't sell his head."

"Sell his *head?*" I cried. "What are you talking about? I won't sleep with a madman."

"Be calm, be calm," said Coffin. "This harpooner has just arrived from the South Seas. He bought a lot of embalmed[12] heads in New Zealand, and now he's trying to sell them. So don't worry."

Then the landlord took me upstairs to the bedroom. It was small and cold, but the bed was big enough for four men to sleep in. There was a large seaman's bag and a tall harpoon standing by the top of the bed. I guessed that both objects belonged to the man I was to share the bed with.

The Man Who Sold Heads

Peter Coffin put a candle on the table in the center of the room. Then he said goodnight and went back to the bar.

I was cold and tired, so I undressed, blew out the candle and got into bed. I was almost asleep when I heard a noise outside the room. I looked up and saw a light under the door.

"It must be the harpooner," I thought. "The man who sells embalmed heads!"

I wanted to hide, or run from the room, but I could not move. My whole body was shaking with fear.

The stranger came into the room. He had a candle in one hand and the embalmed head in the other. Without looking towards the bed, he put the candle in a corner of the room on the floor and opened his bag. All I could see was his black shadow on the wall.

Then, after a moment, he lifted the candle and when I saw his face for the first time, I almost screamed! His skin was colored purple and yellow, with black lines and squares across it. At first I thought he had been fighting and had been badly cut, but then I remembered a story I had heard. It was about a whaleman who had been caught and tattooed[13] all over his body by cannibals in the South Seas. Had it happened to this man too?

The stranger put a hand in his bag and pulled out a tomahawk, then he pulled his hat off his head. There was just a small circle of hair in the center of his bare head. A tomahawk and a wild haircut! What sort of man was this?

I watched, terrified, as he started to undress. I could see that the tattoos covered every part of his body. Then he lifted the tomahawk. I wanted to shout for help, but before I could open my mouth, he put the tomahawk into *his* mouth. Then he lifted the candle to one end of it and blew smoke from between his lips. He was using the tomahawk as a pipe[14]!

Then the man pulled out a strange little figure which was the size of a three-day-old baby. Remembering the embalmed head, I first thought it might be the body of a real child. But then I saw it was a small wooden figure.

*The stranger lifted the candle to one end,
and blew smoke from his lips.*

The Man Who Sold Heads

The man blew out the candle and jumped into the bed. At that moment I screamed—I could not help it.

"What the—!" the man shouted, and tried to catch hold of me.

"Landlord! Peter Coffin! Help me, help me!" I shouted.

"Who are you?" he growled at me. "Tell me, or I'll kill you!"

Suddenly, the door burst open and the landlord ran in. I jumped out of the bed and ran across to him.

"Help me! Help me!" I cried.

"Don't be afraid now," Peter Coffin said, smiling. "Queequeg won't hurt you."

"Why didn't you tell me that I was to share a bed with a cannibal?" I shouted.

"I thought you knew it," said Coffin. "I told you he was selling embalmed heads in the town." He turned to the other man. "Queequeg, this man will sleep here tonight. Is that all right?"

Queequeg nodded calmly and pulled back the bedclothes.

"You get in first," he said to me.

I looked at him. Although he was a cannibal, he seemed clean and respectable, a simple human being like myself.

"Goodnight," said Peter Coffin, and he went out of the room.

I got into the bed again and blew out the candle—and never slept better in my life.

When I woke up the next morning, I found Queequeg's arm round me. He was still asleep.

"Queequeg," I said. He did not move.

I felt something scratch against my leg as I moved away from him. I pulled back the sheet and saw the tomahawk lying next to me. I was in bed with a tomahawk and a cannibal! Was the world going crazy?

"Queequeg!" I said again. "Wake up!"

At last he opened his eyes and sat up in the bed. He looked at me strangely for a moment, then he got out of bed and put on his clothes. When he was dressed, he put some soap on his face and shaved[15]—*with his harpoon!*

Then he walked out of the room with the harpoon in his hand.

I got dressed quickly and followed him down to the bar. It was full of sailors. They were nearly all whalers, or from whaling ships. Chief mates[16], second mates, third mates—officers who only took orders from the captain. Mixed with them were men of every social rank[17]. There were carpenters, whose job it was to repair and make all the wooden things on a ship. There were blacksmiths, who made the harpoons and other weapons. And of course there were the harpooners, those men who hunted and chased and killed the whales.

"Food!" cried the landlord, throwing open the door to the dining room.

We all followed him into the dining room for breakfast. Queequeg and I sat at a table with all the whalers. There were no separate places for officers and ordinary seamen here. All the men were mixed together in a friendly way. Queequeg sat at the top of the table, using his harpoon like a knife. I sat next to him and ate my breakfast in silence.

2
The Pequod

After breakfast, I went out for a walk. Like the docks area of any port, there were sailing men from all parts of the world walking or talking together in the streets.

After about an hour, I came to the Whaleman's Church. It was Sunday, so I went inside and sat near the door. Most sailors will visit a church when they know that they are soon to sail across the ocean. Turning sideways, I was surprised to see Queequeg sitting near me. He was the only person who noticed me enter.

The Pequod

I had not been sitting there very long when the preacher came in. It was the famous Father Mapple, a great favorite of whalemen. When it was time for Father Mapple to speak, he talked about Jonah and the Whale—that famous story about the man who is swallowed by a great whale. Everyone knew the story, of course, but we all listened quietly.

Jonah was a prophet—a person chosen by God to tell the things that God wants people to know. One day, God told Jonah to go to the bad city of Nineveh and preach God's words. But instead of going to Nineveh, Jonah went to Joppa and got on a ship that was going to Tarshish. Soon after they set off, there was a great storm and the ship was in danger of sinking. All the sailors were very afraid. They decided that God had sent the terrible storm to punish Jonah, so they threw him overboard into the sea.

But Jonah did not drown. God sent a great fish—a whale—to swallow him, and Jonah was inside the fish for three days and three nights. Jonah prayed to God to save his life, and God told the whale to spout out Jonah on to dry land. After this, Jonah did as God asked, and he went to Nineveh and preached the words of God.

When the story was finished, I left the church and walked back to the Spouter Inn. I found Queequeg there alone. He had left the church before me and was sitting next to the fire. He was carving a small wooden figure with a knife.

A moment later, he lit the tomahawk pipe, and we were soon passing it between us and sharing a friendly smoke. Then he put his head against mine and put his arm round my shoulders.

"We are friends for life!" he said. "I would die for you!"

After eating a meal together, we went up to our room. Then he took thirty dollars from his bag and gave me fifteen. I started to refuse the money, but he silenced me by putting it into my pocket.

Then he began to talk about himself and I soon learned many interesting things about his life. He was born on the island of

The Pequod

Rokovoko, a place far away to the west and south in the Pacific Ocean which is not on any map. His father was a High Chief—a king. But he was a sick man and when he died, Queequeg would be King. But Queequeg was not ready to return to the island and be King. He wanted to explore the oceans and see the world first.

One day, a whaling ship visited Rokovoko and Queequeg asked the captain to make him a member of the crew. The captain refused because he already had enough sailors. But Queequeg was determined to get on the ship. He took a small boat out to sea and waited. When the ship went past, he climbed up the anchor chains and on to the deck.

"You will have to kill me to make me leave this ship," he told the captain.

After a minute or two, the captain agreed to let Queequeg stay aboard[18]—but only to work as an ordinary sailor. There would be no special treatment because he was the son of a High Chief. Queequeg was happy to agree to this.

"I wanted to learn about different lands and different people," he told me. "Then I planned to go back to my island and teach these things to my own people. I believed I would learn things to make my people even happier and cleverer. But I soon discovered that people everywhere can be both miserable and bad. I realized that they can be far worse than my own people."

I asked him if he was planning to go back to the island, but he said that he was not ready to return yet. He wanted to explore the oceans as a harpooner.

"I want to go whaling too," I said. "I plan to go to Nantucket to find a ship."

"We'll go together," Queequeg replied. "We'll find a ship and share an adventure!"

The next morning, I paid our bill at the inn and we got on the boat for Nantucket island. It was late evening when we arrived. Peter Coffin had suggested we stay at the *Try Pots Inn,* where his cousin was the landlord. We soon found the place and, after a wonderful supper of clam chowder—a thick soup—we went to our beds.

Before sleeping, we spoke about our plans for the next day.

"Yojo has told me that you must choose the whaling ship we sail on," Queenqueg said.

Yojo was the name of his little wooden figure. To Queequeg, Yojo was a little god. He told me that whaleman always believed everything that Yojo told Queequeg. (I never discovered *how* Yojo told him these things.)

"But I know nothing about whaling ships," I said. "I was hoping that you—"

"It will be all right," Queequeg told me. "You will choose the right ship. Yojo is never wrong about these things."

So the next morning I went out to find us a ship. I soon discovered that there were three ships about to sail on three-year voyages. But only one of them, the *Pequod*, was still looking for crew members. She[19] was an old ship, her wooden body dark and weather-stained[20] after years of fighting storms and high seas in oceans around the world.

I went aboard and found an old sailor sitting in a chair on the deck. His face was covered with hundreds of fine wrinkles.

"Are you the captain of the *Pequod*?" I asked him.

"Yes, young man, I am," he said.

"I'm here to sign on as a crew member, to go whaling," I told him.

"And what do you know about whaling?" he asked.

"Nothing," I answered. "But I can learn quickly."

"Have you seen Captain Ahab?" the sailor asked.

"Who is Captain Ahab?"

"The captain of this ship."

"I thought you were the captain," I said.

"I'm Captain Peleg," he said. "The *Pequod* belongs to myself and Captain Bildad. We're responsible for seeing that the ship is

The Pequod

supplied with everything she needs for the voyage. Ahab is the captain of the *Pequod*. He's only got one leg."

"Only one leg?" I said. "Was the other leg lost to a whale?"

"Lost!" Peleg shouted. "Not lost—eaten! Bitten into tiny pieces by the biggest, most terrible whale in all the oceans. A *monster* of a whale!" Then he looked at me for a moment. "Why do you want to go to sea?" he asked.

"I want to see the world," I answered.

"Go to the side of the ship and look out," he ordered.

I was a little puzzled, but I went to the side of the ship and looked out. I stared at the open sea and the horizon.

"Well, what can you see?" Peleg asked.

"Not very much," I replied. "Only water."

"So now you've seen the world," he said. "Do you want to go round Cape Horn and see some more of it?"

"I want to go whaling," I told him.

"Well, I can see you're determined to go," he said.

"I am, sir," I said.

"All right," he said. "You can sign the papers now. Come with me."

He took me below deck to the cabin where a tall, thin man was waiting.

"This man wants to sign up for the voyage, Bildad," said Peleg.

Captain Bildad looked at me. "Do you?" he asked.

"I do, sir," I said.

"So what do you think of him?" Peleg asked.

Bildad stared at me for a long moment. Then he shrugged[21].

"He'll do[22]," he replied.

A whaling crew is paid with a share of whatever profit[23] comes from the voyage. Immediately the two captains began to argue about the size of the share they should pay me. Bildad mentioned an amount but Peleg complained that it was too small.

"You're much too generous, Peleg," shouted Bildad. But after more argument, he agreed to pay me a slightly larger share.

"I've got a friend who wants to go whaling, too," I said. "Shall I bring him to the ship tomorrow?"

"What share does he want?" asked Bildad.

"Oh don't worry about that!" said Peleg as he turned to me. "Has this man ever been whaling before?" he asked.

"Yes, sir," I replied. "He's killed more whales than I can count."

"Well, bring him along," said Peleg.

I signed the papers for the voyage and gave them to Peleg. But as I walked away, I realized that I had agreed to sign up for the voyage without meeting its captain. I stopped and turned back round, feeling suddenly nervous.

"I would like to see Captain Ahab," I said to Peleg. "Where can I find him?"

"Why?" Peleg asked. "You're signed up for the voyage. Anyway, I don't think you can see him. I don't know what's the matter with him, but he stays inside the house."

"Is he sick?" I asked.

"Ahab's not sick, but he's not very well," answered Peleg. "He won't always see me, so I don't think he'll see you. He's a strange man, but you'll like him. He doesn't speak much, but when he does speak it's best to listen."

"Do you know him well?" I asked.

"Yes, I've sailed with him," said Peleg. "He's a good man. He's gone to colleges as well as lived with cannibals, and he's seen many wonderful things. He's the best whaler on the oceans and a fine captain. I know that on his last voyage he acted a little crazy for a while. That was because of the terrible pains in the part of his leg that the whale left behind. He'll be all right when he goes to sea again. Yes, Ahab's a great man, and don't you forget that. Now, goodbye."

3
Elijah's Warning

The next day, I took Queequeg along to the *Pequod* to sign the papers. We were walking away from the ship when a stranger stopped us.

"Shipmates[24], have you signed on as crew for that ship?" he asked.

He was wearing a dirty old jacket and trousers and a black handkerchief tied around his neck. His face was old and his skin was dried from the wind and badly scarred[25] from a past illness.

"Do you mean the *Pequod*?" I asked.

"Yes, the *Pequod*," said the stranger.

"Yes, we've signed on," I said.

"Have you seen Old Thunder yet?"

"Who's Old Thunder?" I said.

"Captain Ahab," he replied.

"The captain of our ship?"

"Yes," the man said.

"No, we haven't seen him," I said. "They say he's sick, but he's getting better. He'll be all right when it's time to sail."

"All right when it's time to sail!" laughed the stranger. "Ha. That's funny! Listen to me. When Ahab is all right then I'll be all right—and not before."

"What do you know about him?" I asked.

"What did they tell *you* about him?" he said.

"Not very much," I replied. "They say he's a good whale-hunter and a good captain to his crew."

"That's true, that's true," said the stranger. "But you must move quickly when he gives an order. Did they tell you what happened to him off Cape Horn? It was a long time ago, but he was like a dead man for three days and nights. Did they say anything about

Elijah's Warning

the fight with the Spaniard? Did they tell you about him losing his leg on the last voyage? Yes, I expect they told you about the leg."

"My friend," I said. "What's all this talk about? Are you a little strange in the head? But if you're speaking about the *Pequod*, then I know all about how Captain Ahab lost his leg."

"*All* about it? Are you sure?" asked the man. He looked back at the ship. "Well, you've signed now, and some sailors must go with him I suppose. But God help them! Good morning, shipmates. I'm sorry I stopped you."

"Listen, friend," I said. "If you have anything important to say, then say it. It's easy for a man to pretend he has a great secret, but you can't trick us."

"Good morning to you, shipmates," the stranger said again, then he smiled and began to move away.

"Wait!" I said. "What's your name?"

"Elijah," he replied.

As we walked away from him, Queequeg and I both agreed that this dirty old sailor was nothing but a troublemaker. But after a short distance I realized that the old man was following us. I said nothing about this to Queequeg, but turned and walked on again. Elijah went past without looking at us. For some minutes after that, I thought about what he had said. Then I decided that he was crazy.

The day after Queequeg signed his papers, a message went out to all the inns. The crew for the *Peqod* must have their bags aboard before night. The ship could be sailing soon. Queequeg and I took our things to the ship, but we decided to sleep ashore until it was time to sail.

A day or two went by, and life was busy aboard the *Pequod*. The old sails were being mended, and new sails, ropes and rigging were coming on board. There were spare whaleboats for chasing the whales, and spare harpoons and lines. Captain Peleg almost never went ashore, and Captain Bildad was busy paying for all the

Elijah's Warning

food and other things that the ship needed for the voyage. Three years is a long time to be away at sea.

During this time, I often went down to the docks to ask about Captain Ahab. I wanted to know how he was and when he was going to come aboard his ship. I was told that he was getting better and was expected aboard soon.

Then, at last, a message came to say that the *Pequod* would sail the next day. So, at six o'clock on a gray, misty morning, Queequeg and I went down to the dock. We were nearing the ship when I saw some figures in the mist.

"There are some other sailors ahead of us, Queequeg," I said.

Before my friend could answer, a voice said, "Ahoy[26] there!" At the same time, a hand came down on both our shoulders. We turned and saw Elijah again.

"Are you going aboard?" he said.

"Yes, we are," I said.

"Did you see some strange men going towards the ship a few moments ago?" he asked.

"Yes," I answered. "I think I saw four or five men, but it was too misty to be certain."

"Very misty, yes. Good morning to you," he finished, and began to move away. Then he turned and whispered, "See if you can find them now."

"Find who?" I asked.

"Good morning to you," he repeated. "I was going to warn you about—but it doesn't matter. I don't expect I'll see you again. Any man who sails on that ship will not return. Goodbye." And then he was gone.

Soon after, we went aboard the ship. Everything was quiet.

"Where did those sailors go, Queequeg?" I said.

"Sailors? What sailors?" said Queequeg.

At last the sun broke through the mist and the crew began to arrive, two and three at a time. We learnt that Captain Ahab was already on board and in his cabin.

At midday, Captain Peleg came from the cabin and spoke to Starbuck, the chief mate.

"Mr Starbuck, are you sure everything is aboard?" he asked. "Captain Ahab is ready. I spoke to him a few minutes ago."

"Everything is aboard, sir," replied Starbuck.

"Then let's go!" cried Peleg.

"Yes, sir," said Starbuck.

Slowly Captain Peleg guided the ship out into the open sea, away from the docks. He was behaving as if he were our captain at sea, rather than Ahab, who had still not appeared. But as it was quite normal for a captain not so show himself until a ship had been at sea for some days, we did not question it.

At last, the anchor was up, the sails set, and we were off!

Our voyage had begun on Christmas Day—a short, northern wintry day that quickly turned dark. Early that first evening, Captain Peleg climbed down into the small boat that would take him back ashore. "God bless you all," he said. "Be careful, and good hunting. I hope you'll have fine weather. Goodbye! Goodbye!"

The ship and the boat went their separate ways. A cold wind blew and a screaming seagull flew over our heads. My adventure had begun!

4
Captain Ahab

Starbuck, the chief mate, was thirty years old and from Nantucket. Next to the captain, he was the most important man on the ship. He was a strong, practical, sensible man with many years of experience at sea.

"I won't have a man in my boat who is not afraid of a whale," he told us. "A man without fear is more dangerous than a coward[27]."

Both Starbuck's father and brother had been killed on whaling trips.

"Starbuck is careful, but he's a brave man, too," Stubb, the second mate, told me. Stubb was from Cape Cod. He was a happy, relaxed sort of man, even when he was chasing whales. He smoked constantly on a short, black pipe. It was only out of his mouth when he slept.

The third mate was Flask. He was a short, red-faced man from Martha's Vineyard. Whales made Flask angry, and he had decided that his job was to kill as many of them as possible.

When a whale was spotted, a number of smaller boats would set off after it. Each boat would each be captained by Starbuck, Stubb and Flask. Each man would carry a whaling spear and would be accompanied by a harpooner.

As well as Queequeg, who would accompany Starbuck when the time came, there were two other harpooners: Daggoo, an African who was six-feet-five tall, and Tashtego, an American Indian. Harpooners were special, brave men who were admired by the other sailors.

For several days after leaving Nantucket, we did not see Captain Ahab. Every time I went on deck I looked for him on the quarterdeck—a place higher than the deck, where the captain stood—but he was not there. It was puzzling[28]. I tried to put the strange Elijah's warnings out of my mind, but it wasn't easy. Then, one cold gray morning, I looked up to the quarterdeck, and there stood Ahab.

He did not look ill, or like a man recovering from illness. He was tall and thin, and he had a white scar down one side of his sunburned face.

At first I didn't notice his white leg. When I did, I saw that it was made from whalebone and fitted into special holes which had been dug into the quarterdeck.

Captain Ahab did not speak. He either stared out at the horizon, or looked down at us with a fierce expression. After only a short time, he went back to his cabin. But after that morning, he came out each day either to stand on the quarterdeck or to walk up and down among the crew.

Spring had arrived. The sky became blue and the weather became warmer. We were now in the Tropics, and Ahab was on the deck or quarterdeck day and night, walking up and down and staring out to sea. We could hear his leg tapping on the deck above us as we tried to sleep.

One day he sent a sailor to fetch his pipe. Then he sat on the quarterdeck and smoked. After a few minutes, we heard him say, "Why doesn't my pipe taste the same? And it doesn't calm me anymore. It doesn't give me any pleasure."

And he threw the pipe overboard into the sea.

A few days later, soon after breakfast, Ahab came on deck and began to walk up and down. He seemed anxious[29], but he did not speak. Hour after hour that day, Ahab walked in silence—up and down, up and down.

"What's he thinking, Flask?" asked Stubb. "He's got some idea in his head."

"Yes, you're right," replied Flask.

When evening came, Ahab called Starbuck across to him.

"Call all the men up on deck," Ahab ordered.

Starbuck was surprised. This order was only usually given when there was some sort of emergency.

"Look-outs!" Ahab shouted up to the men on the masts. "Come down!"

The look-outs were sailors who took it in turns[30] to climb up to the top of the ship's tall masts—the mastheads—and look out for whales.

When the men were all on deck, Ahab continued to walk up and down. He did not speak for some minutes. The men whispered to each other, but Ahab didn't seem to notice. Then he turned and shouted,

"What do you do when you see a whale, men?"

"We shout 'Whale!'" cried the sailors. "Or 'There she blows!'"

"Good," shouted Ahab. "And what do you do next, men?"

"We put the boats over the side of the ship and go after it," answered the men.

Each answer seemed to make Ahab happier.

"All you look-outs and whaleboat captains have heard me give orders about a white sperm whale," said Ahab. Then he held up a gold coin which shone brightly in the sun. "Look at this, men! Do you see it? It's a Spanish gold coin, worth sixteen dollars. Mr Starbuck, fetch me a hammer[31]."

Moments later, Starbuck returned with a hammer. Ahab took it and walked across to the ship's main mast.

"The first man to see a white whale with a wrinkled brow and a crooked jaw gets this gold coin!" he shouted. And he took a nail from his coat pocket and hammered the coin into the mast.

"A white whale, remember," he cried. "Look for white water. If you see him, shout as loud as you can."

Tashtego, Dagoo and Queequeg were listening with more interest and surprise than the others.

"Captain Ahab," said Tashtego. "Do you mean the famous white whale they call Moby Dick?"

"Moby Dick? Do you know the white whale, Tash?" asked Ahab.

"Yes, sir," said Tashtego. "He moves his tail strangely before he goes under the water."

"And he's got a great white spout that sends water high into the sky, Captain," said Daggoo.

"And there are three or more harpoons stuck in him," said Queequeg.

"Yes, that's right, Queequeg," said Ahab. "That's Moby Dick, men."

"Captain Ahab," said Starbuck. "I've heard about this white whale. Was it Moby Dick who took your leg?"

"Who told you that?" Ahab looked angrily at Starbuck for a moment. Then he said, "Yes, Starbuck, it's true. It was Moby Dick who took my leg. And I'll chase him round the Cape of Good Hope and Cape Horn, and across the world before I let him get away! You see, that is what you signed for when you signed for this voyage, men. To chase that white whale all over the earth until he spouts black blood and dies. Will you do that?"

"Yes, yes!" shouted the harpooners. "Death to Moby Dick! Death to Moby Dick!"

"God bless you, men," said Ahab. "But Mr Starbuck, why are you looking so unhappy? Won't you chase the white whale with me? Won't you help me catch Moby Dick?"

"I'll help you catch him, if he comes our way," said Starbuck. "But I'm here to chase whales, not to satisfy the revenge[32] of my captain. Whaling is my business, but how many barrels[33] of oil will your revenge get us? To be angry with an animal is crazy, and— "

"Angry?" shouted Ahab. "Yes, I'm angry. I hate that whale, and I'll kill him! The crew are with me. Are you, Starbuck? Or are you going to go against me? Speak now, if you are."

Ahab waited a moment, then went on, "Ah, you're silent. That gives me your answer."

"God help me," whispered Starbuck to himself. "God help us all!"

5
The Five "Ghosts"

It was night time. I was on deck when I heard two sailors talking.

"Listen! Did you hear that noise, Cabaco?" said one man.

"What noise, Archie?" asked the other man.

"There it is again—below deck! Do you hear it? It's someone coughing," said Archie.

"I don't hear anything," said Cabaco.

"And again!" said Archie. "Listen! It's the sound of two or three men moving in their beds. I think there are some other men hidden below deck, and we haven't seen them yet. And I suspect our captain knows something about it."

After his talk with the crew, our captain had spent most of his nights studying charts and maps. He knew about sperm whales' feeding habits and was able to make quite good guesses at the times and places where he might find Moby Dick.

At the same time, his men told each other many stories about the great white whale. Some were true, some imagined. To believe them all meant that Moby Dick must have been in ten places in the world at the same time.

Already, many men had died trying to catch Moby Dick. One whaling captain had jumped on his back and attacked him with a knife. But the whale had simply turned his great head and bitten off the captain's leg. That man was Captain Ahab. His shipmates had pulled him from the water and he was screaming with pain. For weeks after that, he was like a madman and the crew had to tie him to his bed.

Now this crazy gray-haired old man was chasing the same whale around the world. Would his hatred for Moby Dick drive us all to our deaths?

The Five "Ghosts"

It was a cloudy, warm afternoon. Sailors were half-asleep on the decks or staring out to sea. I was sitting with Queequeg. Suddenly, there was a shout from the top of the main mast.

"There she blows! Whales! Lots of them!" It was Tashtego. He was pointing out to sea with his left hand.

Immediately, every man on the ship began to move. Tashtego came down from the mast and we helped the crew put the whaleboats over the side of the ship.

At that moment, we heard a sound behind us and turned round. Captain Ahab was standing there with five men. They stood like ghosts around Ahab. Then four of them went to one of the spare whaleboats and put it over the side of the ship. The fifth man was the chief of the others. He wore black cotton trousers and a black cotton jacket. He had one white tooth, and his hair was fixed high on his head like a tall hat.

"Are you ready, Fedallah?" Ahab asked him.

"I'm ready," was the whispered reply.

"Then lower the boats!" Ahab shouted.

The other men and I jumped into our three boats and they were lowered quickly into the sea. I was in Starbuck's boat. We were rowing[34] away from the ship when the fourth boat came from the other side of the ship. The five strangers were rowing it, and Captain Ahab stood behind them.

"Move out!" Ahab shouted to the three boats captained by Starbuck, Stubb and Flask. "Spread yourselves!"

"Captain Ahab—?" began Starbuck, staring at the strange men.

"Flask, pull away to your left!" shouted Ahab.

"Yes-yes, sir!" shouted Flask. "Don't worry about the captain's new crew," he told his men. "Row, boys, row! There she blows! There she blows!"

"I heard them!" said Archie. "I heard them below deck, and I told Cabaco."

The Five "Ghosts"

"Did you?" said Flask.

"Yes," Archie replied. "He didn't believe me, but I told him."

Soon Stubb's and Starbuck's boats were passing each other, and Stubb spoke to the first mate.

"Mr Starbuck, sir!"

"Yes, Stubb?" answered Starbuck.

"What do you think about those new men?" asked Stubb.

"They came on board secretly before the ship left Nantucket," replied Starbuck. "I'm sure of it."

"That's what I thought," said Stubb.

"But why are they here?" asked Starbuck.

"It's all because of the white whale," answered Stubb.

The arrival of these five strangers did not frighten the rest of the crew. Archie had already told them about what he had heard, so they were not as surprised as they might have been. But this did not stop them from wondering about them. Where had Ahab found them? How had he persuaded[35] them to come on the voyage? Wild stories would spread about the men, but nobody knew the truth.

I remembered the strange shadows in the mist the day that Queequeg and I had come aboard. "These strangers must be the men I saw," I thought.

Then I remembered Elijah's mysterious warning.

Captain Ahab's boat was far ahead of the others. Fedallah had thrown off his black jacket and now stood holding his harpoon. Suddenly, Ahab put up his hand. It was a signal for every man to stop rowing.

"Queequeg, stand up and look out," Starbuck ordered.

Queequeg stood up in the boat and looked around for the whales. Across from us, Flask was also looking from his boat. For a moment everything had gone silent and still. Then Starbuck suddenly shouted,

"Row, boys, row!"

The Five "Ghosts"

Great waves lifted us up, then threw us down again. The boats separated, and our boat began to chase after three whales. Our sail was up and, with the strong wind, we rushed through the water.

"Pull, boys, pull!" said Starbuck. "We must kill them before the wind gets too strong for us. Stand up, Queequeg!"

Queequeg jumped up at the front of the boat. His harpoon was ready in his hand. We all waited. Then there was a sudden loud noise as one of the whales came up through the waves.

"That's him!" said Starbuck. "Throw, Queequeg, throw!"

Queequeg's harpoon flew out of his hand. Immediately there was a hard push from behind the boat, while the front seemed to hit something hard. The sail crashed down, and something rolled beneath us. The whale had begun to swim quickly away, pulling us behind it as it went, the harpoon stuck in its back. Then a wave of water rushed over and filled the boat. Men and oars were thrown into the sea, but somehow the boat had stayed afloat.

The whale had escaped. Queequeg's harpoon had caused him only a little damage. We swam around the boat and picked up our oars, then climbed back into our places. We were up to our knees in water and the wind was getting stronger. It was nearly dark, and there was a mist. We could not see the *Pequod*.

For more than an hour we fought against the sea and the strong winds as we shouted out to the other boats. But we could not see them and they could not hear us. We were wet, shivering with cold, and tired. Then Queequeg suddenly stood up.

"Listen!" he said.

I heard a chain moving, and the sound of something coming closer to us. Moments later, we saw the shape of the *Pequod* moving slowly through the mist. It was going to hit us!

"Jump, men! Jump!" cried Starbuck. "Get out of the way!"

We all threw ourselves into the sea and began to swim away from the approaching ship, but the waves picked us up and threw us against its sides.

At last our shipmates threw down ropes and helped us climb up into the ship.

"Does this sort of thing happen often, Queequeg?" I asked my friend when I was safely back on deck. I was still shaking with cold and fear.

"Quite often," he told me, without much emotion.

6
"Lower the Boats!"

Days and weeks passed. The weather was calm, and the *Pequod* sailed through several whaling areas and on to the south of St Helena. Captain Ahab's "ghosts" had now come on deck with the rest of the crew. Their leader, Fedallah, spoke to the other strangers, but nobody else. He was a strange man, and a little frightening. Every night he would climb the main mast to be look-out.

It was soon after midnight on one of these quiet moonlit nights that Fedallah shouted "There she blows!" and pointed to the water ahead of him.

Captain Ahab quickly came on deck and called for the sails to be raised. The ship then moved fast through the water, and Ahab jumped up and down on the deck like an excited child. But although almost every man on the ship looked for the whale, they saw it once, but not a second time.

Some days later, again just after midnight, Fedallah shouted, "There she blows!"

And once more, sails were raised and the ship started the chase. But again the whale disappeared. This began to happen night after night. The whale would appear—and then disappear.

But at last we turned to the east, and to the Cape of Good

"Lower the Boats!"

Hope. The Cape of Trouble would be a better name for it! Storms and strong winds began to blow the ship about like a toy on the ocean. It rose into the air, then crashed down on the high waves. Seagulls flew above us, and every morning they sat on the sails and masts.

During this time, Captain Ahab walked up and down the deck, but he did not speak more than a few words to anyone. Instead he would stand for hours, staring out to sea.

One day, as we sailed south-east from the Cape, another whaling ship came towards us out of a sea mist. I was look-out up on a mast at the front of the ship and had a good view of her. The ship was the *Albatross*. Only her lower sails were up, and the clothes of her look-outs were like rags. The men had the long beards and tired faces of sailors who had been at sea for a very long time.

Captain Ahab called to the ship from the quarterdeck.

"Ahoy there! Have you seen the white whale?"

The captain of the *Albatross* shouted a reply, but the wind carried his words away.

Ahab tried again. "This is the *Pequod*. We're sailing round the world. Send all future letters to the Pacific Ocean!"

Ships passing on the oceans of the world usually stop to exchange news, or for their captains to have a meal together. Ships coming from England usually carry letters for the sailors of other ships at sea. But the other ship was already being pushed away from us by the wind.

We sailed north-east, towards the island of Java. The sky was blue, and the sea calm. A gentle breeze was pushing us along. Then, one hot sunny morning, Daggoo was look-out on the main mast. He saw something large and white. Suddenly he shouted,

"There she blows! It's the white whale! It's Moby Dick!"

We looked to where he pointed. In the distance, we could see a great area of white bubbling[36] on the sea's surface. It disappeared, leaving the sea still and calm once more, then reappeared.

"Lower the Boats!"

Could it be Moby Dick? It did not look like a whale.

Captain Ahab was on the quarterdeck. He quickly looked to where Daggoo was pointing and studied the wide, bubbling mass. Then he immediately raised his arm.

"Lower the boats!" he shouted.

Within minutes, all four boats were in the sea. Ahab and his "ghost" men were in the first boat. Quickly, we rowed towards the great white shape, but it disappeared under the water.

We stopped rowing and waited. A short time passed then it suddenly floated up again. It was not a whale. It was a great white body with long arms which curled and twisted in the water. It had no face or expression, there was nothing to say that it was a creature or any form of life.

We stared at the terrible thing for a moment or two more before it finally disappeared under the water.

Starbuck spoke with a wild voice. "I'd rather fight Moby Dick than see that white ghost!" he said.

"What was it?" asked Flask.

"The dead body of a great squid[37]," said Starbuck. "Very few whaling ships see one and return home to tell anyone about it."

The sight of a giant squid is very rare, and some sailors, like Starbuck, believe that the sight of one brings very bad luck. However, it was also known that the sperm whale feeds from the squid. Therefore, Queequeg did not agree with Starbuck.

"When you see a squid," he told me as he pointed his harpoon toward the sea, "you'll soon see a sperm whale."

There was no wind the next day. It was very hot, and the crew of the *Pequod* spent most of the time sleeping. There was not much to see in this part of the Indian Ocean. I was look-out on the mast and found it difficult to stay awake. The other look-outs were sleepy too.

Suddenly, bubbles came up beneath the ship and with a shock I realized that I was staring at a huge sperm whale. It was

It was a great white body with long arms.

"Lower the Boats!"

swimming in the water ahead of us. From the sound of shouting below, I knew that others must have seen it, too. All at once the whole ship was awake again.

"Lower the boats!" shouted Captain Ahab.

As soon as the boats were down, the whale swam away from us. Then he put his tail up in the air and dove under the water.

We waited quietly until the whale rose again.

"There he is!" came a shout.

The whale was closest to Stubb's boat, and the second mate called to his men. "Row, boys! Go after him!"

Tashtego went to the front of the boat, his harpoon in his hand.

"Throw, Tashtego, throw!" shouted Stubb.

I watched the harpoon fly through the air and sink into the whale's side. The "line"—the thick rope tied to the harpoon—went round and round him as he circled and turned. Stubb tried to hold the line between his hands but it moved through his fingers so fast that it burned them.

"Wet the line! Wet the line!" he called.

The line was kept in a wooden box. The man nearest the box began to throw seawater over the rope to cool it.

Now the whale was pulling the boat behind it. It moved so fast that every man held tightly to his seat, afraid of being thrown into the sea. Then Tashtego and Stubb changed places, so that Stubb was now at the front of the boat.

"Pull in! Pull in!" he shouted.

The men began to pull the whale closer to the boat. When they were several feet away, Stubb threw one spear, then another. Blood began to pour out of the great fish.

"Pull up—pull up!" shouted Stubb. "Closer, closer!"

When the whale was finally pulled alongside the boat, Stubb pushed his spear into its heart.

"He's dead, Mr Stubb," said Daggoo, after a minute.

"Yes," said Stubb. "He's dead."

7
"Man Overboard!"

It took all three of our boats to pull the dead whale to the *Pequod*. We had been some distance away when we had killed it. Even with all eighteen of us rowing, it still took several hours to get the huge fish to the ship. It was dark by the time we reached it.

Captain Ahab stared at the whale for some minutes. Then he gave orders to tie it to the side of the ship with chains.

"He can stay there until it gets light," he said.

Then he went to his cabin. He did not seem pleased about the whale. In fact, it seemed to remind him that it did not matter how many other whales we might kill and bring to this ship, we still had not caught Moby Dick. And to Ahab, he was the only whale that mattered.

Early the next morning when it was light, Stubb and Starbuck cut two holes in the side of the whale. Then they pushed two large hooks into the holes and pulled the great fish up until it hung from the side of the ship. This was done with ropes and chains which were fixed to the masts. The whale was so heavy that it almost pulled the *Pequod* over on to its side. The whale was more than sixty-five feet long, and his tail was nineteen feet across. The middle part of his body was about fifteen or sixteen feet high. On each side of his body was a fin, an ear and an eye. His eyes were set twenty or twenty-one feet back from the front of his head. Below his head was the jaw, which was about sixteen feet long. On the lower jaw were the whale's huge ivory[38] teeth.

The next job was to take off the whale's skin and remove his blubber—the fatty stuff under the skin. A harpooner took a long knife and made a hole in the lower part of the whale's body. Then he pushed a large hook into the hole. The hook was slowly

"Man Overboard!"

dropped down into the sea, taking the skin with it. The hook was lowered and raised again and again.

Then Stubb and Starbuck used knives to cut out the whale's blubber. It was like taking the skin off a piece of fruit. As the blubber came off, it was dropped through a door in the deck into the "blubber room". Here, some men waited to roll it up.

Finally, all the hooks were taken out and the whale's head was cut off. Then the body was dropped into the sea where it floated away. Only the head remained, hung on a chain outside the ship.

The sharks quickly came to feed from the whale's body as it floated further and further from the ship. The attack went on for two or three hours. More sharks came to join those already there, until they were too far from the ship for us to see them.

Captain Ahab came from his cabin and stood at the side of the ship. He stared down at the whale's head.

"Speak to me, head, and tell me your secret," he said.

A moment later, a voice shouted, "Ship, ahoy!"

Ahab looked up. "Where is it?" he called to the man on the mast.

"To starboard[39], sir, and coming towards us fast!" the man replied.

"Good, good," said Ahab.

As it got closer, we could see that it was another whaling ship—the *Jeroboam* from Nantucket. We watched as it sailed close to the *Pequod*. Then one of its boats was dropped down into the sea and two men climbed into it. One was the boat's captain. The other was a strange looking man with wild yellow hair and a long coat.

As the boat came towards the *Pequod*, Stubb cried, "It's him! It's Gabriel!"

Stubb was not speaking about the captain of the *Jeroboam*, but of the man with yellow hair, who was rowing the boat. "He's crazy!" Stubb went on. "He tells everyone that he's a prophet[40]. The crew are afraid of him, and the captain is frightened to send

"Man Overboard!"

him ashore because he thinks it will bring the ship bad luck."

Starbuck gave an order for a rope ladder to be dropped over the side for our visitors. But the other captain shouted a warning.

"I am Captain Mayhew," he told Ahab. "Many of our crew have a fever. We don't want to bring the fever aboard your ship. I'll talk to you from this boat."

"I am not afraid of the fever," shouted Ahab. "Tell me. Have you seen the white whale?"

"Beware of the white whale!" Gabriel cried up from the smaller boat. "Think about your whaleboats, holed and sunk! Think about your men, lost or drowned!"

Mayhew looked up at Ahab. "Do you mean Moby Dick?" he asked. "Yes, I can tell you a story about Moby Dick."

"Captain, I warned you about that terrible creature before we left port!" shouted Gabriel. "I warned you against attacking the monster, but you didn't listen to me."

"Tell me what happened," Ahab shouted to Mayhew.

"A year or two after we left Nantucket our chief mate, Macey, saw him," explained Mayhew. "Macey took five men in a boat and went after him. Macey was standing up in the boat, holding his harpoon. He was laughing and shouting wildly at the whale. Suddenly, Moby Dick came up out of the sea and knocked Macey off the boat with his tail. Our mate flew high into the air before he fell into the sea. We never saw him again."

Both men were silent for a moment. Then Ahab said, "Yes, I can believe that."

"Do you plan to hunt the white whale?" asked Mayhew.

"I do," said Ahab.

"Then I wish you luck," said Mayhew. Then Gabriel turned the boat around and rowed him back to the *Jeroboam*.

It was Tashtego's job to remove the valuable oil from the whale's head. I watched as he climbed down from the deck and stepped on to it with a bucket in his hand. Rope had been tied to the bucket

"Man Overboard!"

and Daggoo and another man on the deck above were holding the other end of the rope. Tashtego cut a hole in the whale-head with a sharp knife before dropping the bucket into the hole until it disappeared. A few moments later, he shouted, "Pull up now!" to the men on deck.

As Daggoo and the other man pulled hard on the rope, I watched the bucket come up out of the whale's head. It was filled with white liquid— valuable oil. When the bucket finally reached the deck, the men poured the oil into barrels.

Again and again, the bucket was dropped down into the head, reaching deeper and deeper each time. Then something terrible happened. Tashtego had been holding on to one of the chains that was holding the whale's head at the side of the ship. Suddenly, Tashtego cried out as he slipped and fell into the whale's head!

But worse was to come. The chain was not strong enough to hold Tashtego and the head. Seconds later, the chain broke and the head went crashing down into the sea—with Tashtego inside it!

"Man overboard!" shouted Daggoo.

At the same moment, my brave friend Queequeg dove off the side of the ship with a knife in his hand. There was a splash as he hit the water and disappeared. It was several minutes before we saw him come up again.

"He's got him!" someone shouted.

And it was true. Queequeg was holding on to Tashtego and swimming towards the ship.

Some of the crew jumped into one of the whaleboats. We lowered it quickly and they began to row towards the two men. Then they reached down and pulled them into the boat.

When all the men were back aboard the *Pequod*, Queequeg told us about the rescue.

"I had to cut a hole in the head," he explained. "Then I pulled Tashtego out by his hair."

So we lost the whale's head—but Queerqueg had saved Tashtego!

8
The Jungfrau

Some days later, we met the German ship the *Jungfrau*. It was some distance away, but we watched it turn and come towards us. The ship's captain was named Derick De Deer and he came across to the *Pequod* in a small boat. He was carrying an oil can.

"Ha! He's come to beg[41] for oil," laughed Starbuck. "He needs it for his lamps."

The Jungfrau had not caught any whales on its voyage so far. Captain De Deer had come to ask Ahab's crew to give him oil so that he could have some light in his room.

Ahab went to meet him. While Starbuck filled the oil can, Ahab asked all the usual questions about the white whale. But De Deer could not help. He knew nothing about Moby Dick, and had not seen the great fish.

Ahab was able to give the *Jungfrau's* captain all the oil that he needed, and De Deer began to sail back to his boat. But before he had climbed back aboard his ship, there was a loud shout from the look-outs. A number of whales had suddenly appeared ahead of both ships!

The captain immediately ordered three more German whaleboats to be lowered into the sea. They followed De Deer's boat as it chased after the whales. But the last whale was old and sick and it only had one fin. It could not swim as fast as the others.

By now, the *Pequod's* whaleboats were also in the water. I was with Starbuck. Our boats and the German boats were all moving towards the sick whale. He was the largest and the slowest, so he would be the easiest to catch.

De Deer's boat was leading the chase, but the *Pequod* boats were getting closer with every minute. We were afraid De Deer would get his harpoon in the whale first, and De Deer seemed confident that this would happen. He even turned and laughed, and shook his oil can at us.

"Look at that!" cried Starbuck. "I filled that can only five minutes ago! Now he's using it to laugh at us!"

"Are we going to let him win, men?" Stubb shouted. "Row, boys row!"

At that moment, De Deer threw the oil can at our boat.

"Pull, men, pull!" Starbuck shouted.

Flask was also shouting to the men in his boat. "Catch them! Catch the Germans!"

Slowly the three *Pequod* boats drew closer to De Deer's boat. But he was still ahead of us when one of the men dropped his oar. While the man tried to retrieve his oar, De Deer shouted at him angrily. Starbuck, Stubb and Flask all pulled alongside the Germans in their boats.

The sick whale was ahead of us. He was trying hard to get away, using his one fin to swim. He was frightened, and it was almost sad to watch him. Sometimes he sank below the water for a few moments, then he appeared again.

De Deer's harpooner picked up the longest harpoon in his boat and stood ready to throw it at the whale. At the same moment, Queequeg, Tashtego and Dagoo all stood up with their harpoons. The three *Pequod* harpooners threw at the same time. Their harpoons went over the head of the German and into the whale.

The whale immediately began to splash about in the sea, sending great waves towards us. The three *Pequod* boats knocked against the side of the *Jungfrau* boats as they rushed forward. De Deer and his harpooner were both thrown into the water.

"Don't be afraid, boys!" shouted Stubb, laughing. "You'll be picked up soon. I saw some sharks behind us!"

We chased after the sick whale. It was not a long chase, because the whale was tired and weak. Finally our three lines went round him and he dove under the water.

The Jungfrau

"Be ready, men!" shouted Starbuck. Then we waited in silence for him to surface once more.

Two minutes later, the whale's head rose up out of the water and he began to swim away from us.

"Pull in! Pull in!" shouted Starbuck.

As our boats got closer to him, we could see that the fish was blind. There were pools of blood all around him as he turned over in the water. Then he gave one last weak spout—and died.

Lines were thrown around him from each boat while we waited for the *Pequod* to come near us. When she arrived, more lines were thrown around the whale until he was fixed to the side of the ship with chains.

But the old whale was heavy and the ship began to lean heavily to one side.

"Hold on, *Pequod*! Hold on!" cried Stubb. "Don't be in such a hurry to sink! We must do something men, or we'll lose our ship. Quick, cut the chains!"

Queequeg quickly began to cut the chains with an ax. After a moment, they broke and the whale sank into the sea. Immediately the ship straightened in the water.

We were all sad to lose the old whale, but it was the only thing we could have done to save the ship.

Not long after the old whale sank, we heard a shout from the mastheads of the *Jungfrau*. Immediately the German ship lowered her boats again. But the only spout that we could see came from a Finback whale, which has a spout similar to a sperm whale's. But the Finback swims much too fast for any whaler to catch it. De Deer and his men were chasing after a whale that could not be caught!

Most whaling ships take cargo[42] to add to the profit of the voyage. They stop in China or in New York to sell the goods they have brought with them. But did the *Pequod* have cargo for other ports? No, not Captain Ahab's ship! He had taken only what was needed

The Jungfrau

for himself and his crew to stay out at sea for the whole voyage. Did Ahab go ashore at *any* place? Did he stop to get more food or water? No, he did not.

Ahab's plan was to sail north to the far coast of Japan and catch sperm whales. We would then sail on to the Pacific Ocean during the month when the great white whale might be hunting there for food. Here we expected to find Moby Dick.

As we got closer and closer to Java Head, Ahab told the lookouts to be sure to stay awake. But for a long time they did not see one whale. We had begun to think that there were *no* whales in this part of the ocean.

We had reached the Straits of Sundra, between the islands of Sumatra and Java, when a shout came from the masthead.

"There she blows!"

We looked out to see whale spouts some distance ahead of us. There were not just two or three whale spouts, but hundreds of them.

"Put up more sails!" shouted Ahab. "We need to go faster if we're going to catch them!"

And so the *Pequod* began the chase.

The whales soon realized that a ship was behind them and they began to swim faster. Our harpooners prepared to jump into the whaleboats as soon as we got close. We only needed the strong wind to continue and we might be able to catch a number of the creatures. Perhaps one of them was Moby Dick himself!

Suddenly, Tashtego shouted a warning and pointed behind us. We looked back in surprise to see ten or twelve ships following *us*.

"Pirates[43]!" cried Ahab. "Wet the sails to give us more speed! Pirates are coming after us!"

He began to walk up and down the deck, first looking ahead at the whales, then looking behind him at the pirates. After fifteen or twenty minutes, we were out of the Straits and in open sea. Ahab looked back at the pirate ships, which were now very far in the distance.

"We've left them behind, boys!" he shouted. "They'll not come into open sea. Well done!"

He was right. The pirate ships were turning back. We had escaped.

By now we had grown close to the whales.

"Lower the boats!" Starbuck cried. But as soon as the whaleboats were in the water, the whales immediately gathered in a school[44] and began to swim away at great speed.

"Pull, boys, pull!" shouted Starbuck. "Or we'll lose them."

We rowed hard for the next hour and were almost ready to give up the chase when the whales suddenly seemed to become confused about which way to go. They began to splash about in the sea, their tails high in the water. Instead of staying in a straight line, they started to swim in circles.

Our boats at once separated, each rowing towards one of the whales. In our boat, Queequeg stood ready, harpoon in hand. As soon as we were close to one of the fish, his arm came up and he threw the harpoon into the closest whale. Immediately the creature swam towards the others. He was a big fish and he pulled us along after him.

It is very dangerous to be in the centre of a school of whales, but we had little choice. The whale we had hit swam fast, hoping to shake off the harpoon in his side. All around us, the tails and fins of other whales splashed and made waves that threw our boat from side to side. We were expecting to be knocked into the sea at any moment.

But Queequeg remained calm as he steered the boat through the angry creatures whilst we rowed like crazy men. At last, the whale managed to shake Queequeg's harpoon out of his skin and our boat slowed to a stop.

We found ourselves in the center of the school. The water here was flat and calm, like a lake. A great "wall" of whales surrounded us, and there was no way through it. We decided to stay in the center of the lake and, after a few minutes, began to be visited by

The Jungfrau

the cows and their young calves. They swam alongside our boat, touching it with their bodies.

Queequeg put a hand down and touched their heads. Starbuck did the same. And under the water, we could see the mothers who were waiting to give birth to calves. It was wonderful to see all of this, and something that I would never forget.

Suddenly, the calm water around us was full of waves and our boat started to rock from side to side. Moments later, a great whale burst through the water with a harpoon line twisted round his tail. His sudden appearance frightened the other whales and they began to swim in every direction.

"Oars! Oars!" Starbuck whispered. He spoke quietly because he did not want to frighten those creatures closest to us.

The "wall" had broken open now. The whales were swimming in all directions. We rowed quickly but carefully between their bodies. After some minutes, we were back in the open sea again.

Flask killed one whale, but that was all we would catch that day. We rowed back to the *Pequod*, disappointed by our morning's work.

"These things often happen," Queequeg told me. "The more whales you see, the fewer you catch."

*Under the water, we could see the mothers who were
waiting to give birth to calves.*

9
The Rose-bud

A week or two after this, the sailors aboard the *Pequod* began to complain about a bad smell. It was the middle of the day and the weather was calm. Soon a French whaling ship appeared ahead of us with a dead whale hanging from her side. The whale had not been killed, but had died of some sickness. This explained the terrible smell.

The oil from a whale that has died days or weeks earlier is of poor quality and most captains of a whaling ship would have left the creature in the sea. But as we came closer to the French ship, we could see a second whale was hanging to it. The bad smell from this one was even stronger. It was a dry whale—one that has dried up and died from some mystery illness.

We were growing closer to the French ship when Stubb suddenly shouted,

"Look! That's my harpoon stuck in the side of that whale! He's the one that got away from me the other week. Well, there's not enough oil to fill an oil can in either of those creatures. But there could be something more interesting—ambergris! Let's go and look."

Ambergris is very valuable because it is very rare. It is used to make perfumes and candles and can also be used for cooking. It is a thick white substance which is found in the stomachs of sick whales. Whether ambergris causes—or is caused by—that sickness, nobody really knows.

Stubb called to his boat crew, and minutes later they were rowing quickly towards the French ship. Later that day, one of Stubb's crew who could speak French and overheard everything, told me the story.

The Rose-bud

The ship was called *Bouton de Rose,* or the *Rose-bud* in English.

"A Rose-bud?" said Stubb, laughing. "She doesn't smell like a rose, that's for certain!"

The boat crew pulled closer to the ship and Stubb shouted to the men on board,

"Ahoy, there! Do any of you Rose-buds speak English?"

"I do," shouted one of the men on deck.

"Who are you?" aaked Stubb.

"I'm the chief mate," answered the man.

"Well, my little Rose-bud," called Stubb. "Have you seen the white whale?"

"The *what* whale?"

"The white whale—a great sperm whale called Moby Dick. Have you seen him?"

"I've never heard of him," replied the chief mate.

"All right," called Stubb. "Just wait there and I'll be back in a minute."

Stubb's crew quickly rowed back to the *Pequod* where Captain Ahab was waiting on the quarterdeck.

"Well?" he asked Stubb. "Any news of Moby Dick?"

"No, captain," Stubb told him. "They haven't seen him and they've never heard of him."

A disappointed Ahab went back to his cabin. Then Stubb's crew rowed quickly back to the *Rose-bud* where the chief mate had climbed down the chains and was getting ready to cut into the whale. He was holding a bag over his nose.

"What's the matter with your nose?" Stubb asked him. "Have you broken it?"

"I wish it was broken," the chief mate answered, angrily. "I wish I didn't *have* a nose. It would make the job easier. Now, what do you want? I don't have time to stand here talking."

"Don't be angry, Rose-bud," said Stubb. "Stay calm. But you're a fool to think that you can get oil out of that dry whale. You'll be lucky to get a spoonful."

"I'm not a fool, and I know there's little or no oil in this dead fish," replied the chief mate. "But our captain won't believe it. This is his first voyage and he won't listen to anything I tell him."

"I'm sorry to hear that," said Stubb.

The chief mate stared at Stubb thoughtfully for a moment. Then he said,

"Why don't you come aboard?"

"Me?" said Stubb. "Now?"

"Yes," said the chief mate. "Perhaps the captain will listen to you. Come and speak to him."

"I'll be happy to help," said Stubb, smiling. And he and two of his crew climbed aboard the ship.

The sailors on the *Rose-bud*'s deck wore red caps and were getting ready to cut up the whales. They covered their noses with their hands as they worked. Some of them smoked pipes to cover the terrible smell. Every minute or two, a man would climb up the mast for some fresh air. As soon as he was down, another man would climb the mast for the same reason.

The chief mate met Stubb on the deck. But before either man could speak, the captain's cabin door crashed open. A man ran out and shouted at the chief mate in French, then he turned and ran back inside.

"What was all that about?" asked Stubb.

"That was the ship's doctor," said the chief mate. "He's told the captain we'll all get sick from the whale's smell. But the captain won't listen to him."

"Why not?" asked Stubb.

"Because the man's a fool!" replied the chief mate. "I never want to sail with him again."

For the next few minutes Stubb and the chief mate discussed how they might persuade the *Rose-bud*'s captain to cut free the two dead whales. During all this talk, Stubb quickly realized that

The Rose-bud

the chief mate had not thought about the possibility that the whales might contain ambergris. This pleased him.

Just then, a small man came out of the captain's cabin. He wore a pretty red coat and had a small beard.

"This is our captain," the chief mate told Stubb. "He doesn't speak English. What should I say to him?"

Stubb tried not to laugh. "Tell him anything you like that may make him get rid of those whales," he said. "Start by telling him that he looks too pretty to be a sailor."

The chief mate smiled at Stubb, then turned to the captain and spoke quickly in French.

"Only yesterday this man met a ship with a dry whale," he said. "The ship's captain, first mate and six sailors had all died from a fever—a fever caught from the smell of a dead dry whale."

The captain began to look frightened.

"What next?" the chief mate asked Stubb.

"Tell him a monkey would make a better captain of the *Rose-bud*," said Stubb. "Tell him that I think *he's* a monkey."

The chief mate turned towards the captain again.

"This man says we must cut the chains from these whales and let them go," he said. "If we don't, we'll all be dead within a week!"

Immediately, the captain ran forward and shouted to the men closest the chains to cut them. Then he returned to Stubb and the chief mate.

"What should I tell him now?" the chief mate asked Stubb.

"Tell him he's been fooled," said Stubb. Then he whispered to his own men, "And he's not the only one."

The chief mate spoke to the captain. "This man was pleased to help us," he said.

The captain said something, then the chief mate turned to Stubb.

"He said he'd like you to drink a glass of wine with him," he told him.

The Rose-bud

"Say thank you, but I never drink with a man I've fooled," said Stubb. "Tell him that I must go."

The chief mate turned to the captain again. "He says there's no time for drinking. We must cut the whales loose at once. Then we must lower our boats and pull the ship away from them."

By this time, Stubb and his two men were climbing back down to their own boat. Stubb turned to the first mate.

"We can help you," he shouted. "We've got a long line, so we can pull the lighter whale away from the ship's side."

"Thank you!" shouted the chief mate.

So while the Frenchman's boats were busy pulling the ship one way, Stubb's boat pulled the smaller, dried-up whale the other way. Then the *Pequod* moved between the French ship and Stubb's boat. Immediately Stubb ordered his men to pull the whale up to the boat.

When it was close enough, Stubb used a knife to cut into the creature. He cut just behind the fin, then began to dig into its stomach with a small spade. The boat crew got excited. Screaming sea birds flew down around them as Stubb worked quickly. The smell was terrible, but then, suddenly, a sweeter smell rose from the insides of the whale.

"I've got it! I've got it!" cried Stubb.

He dropped his spade and pushed his hands into the whale. After a moment, he pulled them out again. In them was something that looked like soft soap or soft cheese.

"Ambergris!" cried Stubb. "Beautiful ambergris! Worth its own weight in gold! All those fine ladies don't realize that their lovely perfumes begin in the stomach of a whale!" he added, laughing.

Six handfuls of ambergris came from the whale, but even more was lost in the sea when Ahab ordered Stubb to stop.

"Come back aboard," Ahab shouted to him impatiently. "Or we'll leave you behind."

10

The Samuel Enderby

Not all of the *Pequod's* crew go in the whaleboats when a whale is spotted. Those that are left behind are called the "ship-keepers". They work on the ship while the boats are chasing the whale. One of our ship-keepers was a young boy named Pip. He was a happy, pleasant member of the crew and everyone liked him.

Soon after the ambergris adventure, one of Stubb's whaleboat men injured his hand, so Pip took the man's place in the boat. He was very nervous on his first trip but it went well, and Pip felt happier when he arrived back on the ship.

On Pip's second trip, his boat was chased by a whale which had been hit by Tashtego's harpoon. The whale turned quickly— and knocked the side of the boat next to Pip. Terrified, the young boy jumped up out of his seat and the next moment he was in the water.

Worse was to happen. The rope became tangled[45] around Pip's body and as the whale began to swim away, it began to drag Pip along behind him.

Tashtego stood watching at the front of the boat. He was full of excitement for the hunt and Pip's accident had made him angry.

"Stupid boy!" he shouted. "If I cut the rope, I'll lose my whale!"

"Cut it!" shouted Stubb. He knew he had to save the boy, but he was angry too. "Cut the rope, Tashtego. Damn[46] him!"

So Tashtego cut the rope and Pip was saved. Minutes later, Stubb pulled him back into the boat.

"Never jump out of a boat again," Stubb told him. "Next time, we'll leave you in the water. That whale was more valuable than you."

The Samuel Enderby

But Pip *did* jump again. It was on the next trip. Again, the whale hit the side of the boat and frightened him. Again, he jumped up out of his seat and into the sea. But this time, Stubb left him in the sea and went after the whale instead. After only three minutes, there was more than a kilometer of open sea between Pip's body and Stubb's whaleboat.

"Help me!" Pip cried. "Come back!"

But Stubb's boat did not turn back. Perhaps Stubb expected one of the other whaleboats to stop and pick up the boy. They did not. They were too busy chasing their own whales to notice him in the water.

Luckily, men on the *Pequod* did see him, and rescued him. But Pip was never the same boy after that day. Every day, he would walk around the ship talking to himself and thanking God for his rescue. The experience had made him go crazy.

"Ship, ahoy! Have you seen the white whale?" shouted Captain Ahab. He was standing in his whaleboat, fixed to the side of the ship. It was some days later, and we had met an English ship called the *Samuel Enderby*.

The captain of the other ship sat comfortably in the front of his own whaleboat. He was a large, handsome man, about sixty years old. He wore a nice blue uniform.

"What did you say?" he called to Ahab.

"Have you seen the white whale?" Ahab said again.

In response, the other captain held up a piece of whalebone where his arm should have been. There was no hand or fingers at the end of it, only the shape of a hammer head. "Have you seen this?" the man shouted.

"Quick, Starbuck!" called Ahab. "Get your men in my boat and take me across to the *Samuel Enderby*."

In less than a minute, we were rowing our captain towards the other ship. But when we reached it, Ahab realized that he had a problem. In his hurry to speak with the other captain, he had

The Samuel Enderby

forgotten something. On the *Pequod* there was a special seat and ropes to get him aboard. There was no special seat on the *Samuel Enderby*. How was he going to get up on to the deck?

Two officers from the English ship dropped a rope ladder over the side. But this was no help to Ahab. The captain looked down and immediately understood the problem.

"Lower the hook, boys!" he cried.

Luckily, the *Samuel Enderby* had caught a whale a day or two earlier. The blubber hook was still hanging outside the ship. It was clean and dry now. We watched it come down. When it reached our boat, Ahab sat over the curve of the hook.

"Bring him up, boys!" said the English captain.

Carefully, our captain was lifted on to the ship and on to the quarterdeck where the English captain was waiting for him.

"Let's shake bones together," said Ahab. He lifted his whalebone leg and knocked it against the Englishman's whalebone arm. The two men laughed.

"Now, where did you see the white whale? How long ago was it?" asked Ahab.

The Englishman pointed his ivory arm towards the east. "I saw him on the Equator[47], last season," he said.

"And he took your arm off?" said Ahab.

"Yes, he was the cause of it. Did he take your leg?"

"Don't worry about my leg," said Ahab. "Tell me your story. What happened?"

"It was the first time in my life that I'd sailed along the Equator," explained the Englishman. "I knew nothing about the white whale at that time. I hadn't heard about him. One day we lowered our boats to chase four or five whales, and my boat went after one of them."

"Go on, go on!" said Ahab, impatiently.

"Our harpooner got a line in him, but the whale went round and round in circles," the man went on. "It was hard for our boat to stay afloat as he pulled us along. Then, suddenly, this great

The Samuel Enderby

head came up out of the water. A huge, milky-white head."

"That's him!" cried Ahab, excitedly. "That's Moby Dick!"

"He had several harpoons sticking in him near one of his fins."

"Yes, they were *my* harpoons!" said Ahab. "Go on, go on."

The Englishman laughed. "I will if you'll let me," he said. "Be patient! Well, this great fish with the white head began biting through my harpooner's line."

"Yes, that's one of his tricks," said Ahab. "He wanted to free the other whale."

"I don't know how it happened, but the line got caught in his teeth," said the Englishman. "We didn't know it then, of course. But when I ordered my men to pull in the line, he came up out of the water and we were on his back! Well, we had lost our other whale, so I decided to catch this one. He was the biggest sperm whale I'd ever seen in my life."

"He's the biggest, yes. What did you do?" asked Ahab.

"I jumped into my first mate's boat, which was beside us," said the Englishman. "Then I picked up a harpoon and stuck it into the white whale's side. The next moment, my eyes were full of seawater. The whale's tail was splashing wildly around us. Suddenly, it crashed down on our boat and smashed it into two pieces! We were all thrown into the water. I got hold of my harpoon, but the whale dove under the water and the waves washed me off his back. Then my arm caught in one of the old harpoons in his side." He put his hand on his shoulder. "It caught me here and was pulled all the way along my arm, cutting it open."

Then he turned to another man who was on the quarterdeck.

"This is Bunger," he said, "our ship's doctor. Tell the captain about my cut, Bunger."

The doctor was a round-faced man. He spoke carefully.

"It was very bad. I did everything I could to save Captain Boomer's arm, and—"

"Oh, yes," interrupted Captain Boomer, with an unpleasant

The Samuel Enderby

smile. "Everything! He drank hot rum with me every night!"

"I sat with Captain Boomer every night—"

"Until he was too drunk to stand up," said Boomer.

"Excuse me, Captain," said the doctor. "I never drink— "

"Water!" interrupted the captain. "You never drink water, only rum. But go on, Doctor. Finish your story."

"Yes, I will," said the doctor, coldly. "The arm got worse and worse. The cut was very deep and very long. When it turned black, I knew that the arm had to come off. But I had nothing to do with the captain's ivory arm. He ordered the ship's carpenter to make it. He wanted that hammer put on the end of it."

"But what happened to the white whale?" asked Ahab.

"We didn't see him again for some time," said Captain Boomer. "It was several weeks later that I first heard stories about him. Then I realized that it was Moby Dick who took my arm."

"Did you see him again?" asked Ahab.

"Yes, twice," said Boomer.

"Could you get a harpoon in him?"

"I didn't want to try," said Boomer. "To lose one arm is bad enough, I don't want to lose the other. No more white whales for me. It would be wonderful to catch him. And there's a lot of valuable sperm oil in him. But it's best to leave him alone." He looked at Ahab's ivory leg. "Don't you agree, captain?"

"It's best, yes," said Ahab. "But he'll still be hunted, despite that. Now, where did you last see him? How long ago? Where was he going?"

The doctor began to walk around Ahab. "Are you sick, sir?" he said. "Let me look at you. Your face is very red, and your blood—"

"Go away!" cried Ahab. And he pushed the doctor away from him. "I must get back to my ship. Which way was Moby Dick going when you last saw him, Boomer?"

"Good God!" cried the English captain. "What's the matter with you? Are you crazy?"

"Tell me!" said Ahab, wildly.

"He was going east, I think," replied Captain Boomer.

Ahab was already sitting in the hook. "Lower me into my boat," he shouted to the ship's sailors.

Moments later he was standing in our boat. Captain Boomer continued to shout warnings to him about the white whale, but Ahab did not listen.

He turned away from the *Samuel Enderby* and looked ahead to his own ship.

"Forward, boys!" he ordered.

11
Queequeg's Coffin

When Ahab jumped down into the boat from the hook of the *Samuel Enderby*, he landed heavily and damaged his ivory leg. When he was back aboard the *Pequod*, he called for the ship's carpenter.

"Make me a new leg," he ordered. "Be sure to choose the best ivory from the whales we've caught on this voyage."

"Yes, yes, sir," said the carpenter.

"Have it ready for me by tonight," said Ahab.

After carefully measuring Ahab's leg, the carpenter went away.

The next morning, Starbuck came to the captain's cabin and found him with a new snow-white ivory leg. We were now in the South China Sea and Ahab was looking at maps and charts when Starbuck knocked on his cabin door. I was working nearby and heard everything that was said.

"Who's there?" called Ahab.

"Starbuck, Captain," said Starbuck.

"Get back on deck," said Ahab. "I'm busy."

Queequeg's Coffin

"We're losing oil from the barrels," said Starbuck. "We must stop and check them."

"Stop?" said Ahab, angrily. "When we are so close to Japan? Waste a week checking a lot of old barrels? No!"

"Either that, or we waste more oil in one day than we can get in a year," said Starbuck. "We've come twenty thousand miles to get it. Surely it's worth saving."

"We're not going to stop," said Ahab. "We can lose the oil, I don't care."

"What will the ship's owners say?" said Starbuck.

"The owners can stand on Nantucket beach and shout as loud as they like," said Ahab. "I'm captain of this ship. You take orders from me, Starbuck. Now, get back on deck."

The chief mate's face was red with anger. "Captain," he said. "You're wrong to—"

"Stop!" shouted Ahab. Then he picked up his gun from the table and pointed it at Starbuck. "I ordered you to get back on deck! Are you refusing to take orders from me?"

Starbuck stepped out of the cabin and stopped by the door.

"You should be careful, Captain," he said. "Not of me, but of yourself... Be careful of Captain Ahab."

And he went away.

For a while after the chief mate had gone, Ahab walked up and down in his cabin. "Be careful of yourself," I heard him say to himself. "Be careful of Ahab. Starbuck is a brave man to speak to me like that. Perhaps he is right. Perhaps I should listen to him. Anyway, I don't want to make the crew angry. I need them to help me catch the white whale."

Some minutes later, he walked up on to the deck and across to the chief mate. "You're a good man, Starbuck," he said. Then he called to the rest of the crew. "Take down the sails! We're going to check the barrels."

We began the work immediately. It was hot, dirty work, and it went on for hours. Queequeg was the man who at last found the

Queequeg's Coffin

barrel with the hole in it. He had been working in the hottest, wettest part of the ship's cargo room. When he came up on deck, he looked sick.

Within two days, he had a bad fever. I stayed beside his bed for as long as I could, and watched him grow thinner and thinner. There were dark circles around his eyes and his bones seemed to show through his tattooed skin. We were all expecting him to die. He expected it, too.

One day he said to me, "When a whaler dies in Nantucket, they put him in a long wooden box."

"You mean a coffin," I said.

"The box is like a boat," he said. "On my island, we put dead men into a boat and send them out to sea. They go to the place where the stars in the sky meet the sea. I don't want to be fed to the sharks when I die, Ishmael. Tell the carpenter to build me a coffin-boat."

"I will, my friend," I said.

I immediately went to see the ship's carpenter and told him what Queequeg wanted.

"All right," he said. "I'll do it."

The old man went to find some thick pieces of wood, then he measured Queequeg's body. For the next hour or two, the carpenter worked on what we all thought would be Queequeg's coffin. When it was finished, he put it on his shoulders and carried it up on deck.

"Is it needed yet?" he asked me and the other men.

"No, it's not," I told him. "But it will be soon."

Queequeg overheard us talking. "Let me see it!" he shouted from his bed.

The carpenter carried the coffin to Queequeg and put it next to his bed. I and some of the crew followed behind him.

Queequeg stared at the coffin for several minutes. Then he said, "Bring me my harpoon and an oar from my whaleboat, Ishmael."

I did this, and he asked me to put them in the coffin.

Queequeg's Coffin

"Now bring some food and some water, and put that in the coffin too," said Queequeg.

When someone had done this, he asked us to put him in the coffin as well. "I want to see if it's comfortable," he said.

So we lifted him into the coffin and he lay there for several minutes without moving. Then he said, "Bring me Yojo."

I fetched the little wooden figure and gave it to him. He held it in his hands.

"Now put the coffin lid on," he ordered. The carpenter did this. One end of the lid opened like a little door, so we could see Queequeg's face.

After a minute or two, he said, "You can put me back in my bed now."

As soon as we did this, young Pip came up to the bed. He was crying quietly. "Where are you going, dear friend?" he asked Queequeg. "Are you going on your last journey? Will you do something for me? Will you look for Pip? He's been missing for a long time. If you find him, be kind to him. He must be very sad. Now, Queequeg, die!"

Starbuck was watching the boy. "Poor Pip," he said to himself. "He says the strangest things since the day we pulled him out of the sea." And he took Pip away.

All this time, Queequeg had been lying with his eyes closed. Now, suddenly, he opened them.

"I've decided not to die," he said. "There is something I must do on my island first."

I stared at him. "Can you really choose whether you are going to live or die?" I asked.

"Certainly," he replied. "Sickness can't kill a whaler if he doesn't want to die. Only a whale or a sinking ship can do that."

Queequeg quickly recovered. Within a few days, the fever left him and he began to eat and drink again. And the coffin? It was tied to the stern of the ship and he used it to keep all his things in.

We sailed on into the calm Pacific Ocean. Ever since I was

Queequeg's Coffin

a boy, it was my dream to sail across the Pacific, and I was very excited. Captain Ahab stood on the quarterdeck like an iron statue, looking eastwards. He was not excited by this endless stretch of blue sea. The Pacific Ocean meant only one thing to him. It was here that his hated white whale was most likely to be swimming. It was somewhere here that the fight to catch Moby Dick would begin.

―――――

Not all whalers know about Moby Dick. The ones who do tell wild stories about a monster who can be seen in many different oceans at the same time. They describe a creature who is thirsty for human blood, who is different from other sperm whales with his snow-white forehead and high white hump. Moby Dick's tail is more than fifty-two feet across. He uses it to push himself along, and as a weapon in his battles with the whaleboats.

You can find many pictures of sperm whales, but few of them are completely accurate[48]. How can they be? Most have been painted by people who have never seen a sperm whale. Most of those who have will have only seen the creature after it has been killed, and a dead sperm whale looks quite different from a live one. Like the difference between a wrecked ship and one still afloat. The only way of knowing what a living, breathing sperm whale *really* looks like is to go whaling yourself. But to do so, you risk your life. So perhaps it is best not to be too curious about them.

12
Ahab's Dream

Perth was the blacksmith on the *Pequod*. He was nearly sixty years old, and he had a thick beard and sunburnt skin. He worked at his anvil[49] on the deck near the main mast. The harpooners brought their weapons to him to be sharpened or repaired.

It was the middle of the day when Ahab walked towards Perth. The captain was carrying a small leather bag. He stopped a short distance away from the blacksmith and watched him for several minutes. Perth worked steadily. He was hitting a red hot piece of iron on his anvil. Sparks flew out every time he hit the metal with his hammer. Some of the sparks flew near Ahab.

"The sparks burn the skin, Perth," said Ahab. "But you live and work among them and they don't burn you."

"Yes, sir," said Perth.

"Why is that?" asked Ahab.

"After years of working at an anvil I'm burned all over, Captain Ahab," replied the blacksmith. "And it's not easy to burn a scar."

"What are you making?" asked Ahab.

"I'm repairing an old whaling spade, sir," answered Perth.

"Can you make it flat and smooth again?" asked Ahab.

"I think so, sir," said Perth.

"And can you make very hard metal smooth again?" asked Ahab.

"Yes, sir, I think I can," said Perth.

Ahab moved closer to the blacksmith. Then he put his hands on Perth's shoulders. "Look here," he said. "Look at the lines in my forehead. Can you smooth away these worried lines? If you can, I'll happily lay my head on your anvil and feel your heaviest hammer smash between my eyes. Can you do it?"

Ahab's Dream

"That's the one thing I can't make smooth, sir," said Perth.

"Yes, blacksmith, that's the answer I expected," said Ahab. "Nobody can make it smooth. You can only *see* the lines on my forehead, but they go deeper. Deep into the bones of my head. But that's enough talk about things that are impossible. And no more spades for you to repair today, Perth. I want you to make me a harpoon that's so strong it will stick in a whale like one of its own fin bones." Ahab shook his leather bag. "These are the nails from the shoes of race horses. Make my harpoon from these."

"Horseshoe nails?" said Perth. "They are made out of the best and hardest metal a blacksmith can work with."

"I know that, old man," said Ahab. "Begin now, and I'll watch you. First make twelve rods[50]. Then twist and hammer them into one strong shaft for the harpoon. Quickly, now! I'll work the fire for you."

When at last the twelve rods were ready, Ahab looked carefully at them. Perth was going to make the shaft when Ahab stopped him.

"I'll do it," said Ahab. And he hammered the rods together on the anvil.

"Captain Ahab," said Perth. "Is this the harpoon for the white whale?"

"Yes it is! It's for the white monster!" cried Ahab. "Next we'll make the blade head. Here are my razors[51], Perth. They're made from the finest steel. Make the barbs[52] for the harpoon blade from them. They have to be as sharp as ice."

The blacksmith looked at the razors for several seconds.

"Take them," said Ahab. "I don't need them. I don't shave now."

So the blacksmith took the razors and used them to make a blade for the harpoon.

"Move the water bucket closer, sir," he told Ahab. "I need heat *and* cold water to make the metal strong."

"No, not ordinary water!" said Ahab. "Not for *this* harpoon.

Ahab's Dream

Ahoy there! Tashtego, Queequeg, Daggoo! Will you give me enough of your blood to cool this blade?"

The three men nodded and moved forward eagerly. Then the captain made cuts in their arms and their blood dripped over the harpoon blade and cooled it. Then Ahab tied some rope between the mast and the side of the deck. He pulled it tight and checked it from end to end. There were no weak places in the rope.

"Good," he said. "Only the best line will do for this harpoon."

Minutes later the harpoon and line were finished, and Ahab walked away with his weapon. We listened to the sound of his ivory leg beating against the wood of the deck.

The *Pequod* went deeper and deeper into the Japanese whaling seas. Soon we were busy catching a great number of whales. Often in calm, pleasant weather the men on the whaleboats worked for twelve, fifteen, eighteen and twenty hours without stopping. I was in Starbuck's boat. We rowed steadily after the whales, or waited quietly for them to appear from out of the sea.

But it was satisfying work. And the Pacific Ocean was a beautiful place to be on the days when a golden sun shone down on us.

A few weeks after Ahab had made his harpoon, we saw a Nantucket ship, the *Bachelor*. She was on her way home to America. The three men at the top of her mast wore bright red cloth in their hats. Flags flew from the masts and rigging.

As the ship sailed towards us, we heard the sound of drums coming from her. And on the quarterdeck, we could see sailors dancing with beautiful girls who had run away with them from the Polynesian Islands. The music for the dancing came from a boat which was tied between two masts. In it were three men playing fiddles made from whale ivory.

Barrels of sperm oil seemed to hang from every part of the ship. Later, we learned that the *Bachelor* had sailed in the same seas as many other ships—some of those ships had gone for months without catching a whale. But the *Bachelor* had been wonderfully lucky. Her whalers had caught hundreds of whales, and they had used every barrel on the ship for the valuable sperm oil. Then every spare piece of wood on the ship was made into barrels to take more of the oil. The sailors' boxes, the cook's cooking pots, coffee pots—everything was used to take the oil.

The ship's captain stood on the quarterdeck. He smiled happily as he watched and enjoyed all that was happening. He had a wine glass and a bottle in his hands. When he saw Captain Ahab standing on the quarterdeck of the *Pequod*, he lifted both objects into the air.

"Come aboard, come aboard!" he shouted to Ahab.

"Have you seen the white whale?" was Ahab's reply.

"No, I've only heard stories about him," said the other man. "And I don't believe them!"

"Have you lost any of your men?" asked Ahab.

"Only two islanders, that's all," replied the other captain. "Now, come aboard and I'll take that worried look from your face. We've got a full ship, and we're on our way home!"

But Ahab refused to go. "I've got an empty ship," he answered. "You go your way, and I'll go mine." Then he ordered full sail into the wind, and the two ships sailed in opposite directions. We, the crew on the *Pequod*, watched the happy faces on the *Bachelor* until they were too far away to see. They were much too busy enjoying themselves to watch us in return.

―――

Sometimes, when you sail past a lucky ship, some of that luck will come to you. So it seemed to the *Pequod*. The day after we met the *Bachelor*, we caught four whales. Ahab caught one of them himself.

It was late afternoon when we finished. We brought three of the whales back to the ship before it became too dark to see what we were doing. The fourth whale was too far away from the ship and we had to leave him until the morning. The men on the boat who had killed him had to stay by his side all night. It was Ahab's boat.

Ahab put a lamp on the whale's back. Then he and most of his crew went to sleep, but not Fedallah (and not the man who told me the story later).

Ahab woke up suddenly and saw Fedallah watching him with his cold black eyes.

"I've dreamed it again," said Ahab.

"You dreamed of hearses[53] and coffins?" asked Fedallah, quietly.

"Yes!" cried Ahab. "My hearse. My coffin."

"I've told you before, old man, you won't have a hearse or a coffin," said Fedallah.

"I won't?" said Ahab.

"No, and you won't die until you have seen two hearses on the sea," said Fedallah. "The first hearse will *not* be made by human hands. The second will be made from wood from a tree that was grown in America."

"Yes, yes!" said Ahab. "It will be a strange thing—hearses floating on the sea. It's not something we'll see soon."

"Believe me, you cannot die until you see them, old man," said Fedallah. "And I will die before you and show you the way."

"I believe everything that you say," said Ahab. "But I will not die before I kill Moby Dick!"

"And only rope can kill you, old man," said Fedallah.

"Rope?" said Ahab. He laughed. "A hangman's[54] rope? On land? Then I'll live forever!"

Both men were silent after this. Slowly, the sky became lighter and the rest of the boat crew woke up. Some hours later, they brought the dead whale to the ship.

13

The Typhoon

The Pacific Ocean can be calm and beautiful one minute, and in the middle of a storm the next. And the worst of these storms are called typhoons. Typhoons burst out of a clear blue sky when you least expect it.

Towards the evening of that day, the sails of the *Pequod* were blown about by the strongest winds I've ever known. Lightning split the black sky, and seconds later the sound of thunder exploded around us like a bomb.

Starbuck stood on the quarterdeck. With every flash of lightning, he looked up to see the wind tear another sail from its mast and blow it out into the darkness. Stubb and Flask shouted to us to lift and tie the whaleboats higher, away from the roaring sea that was beating against the sides of the ship. We did this, but Ahab's whaleboat did not escape damage. A huge wave crashed against the boat's bottom and tore a great hole in it.

"It's bad!" Stubb shouted to Starbuck. "But who can stop a typhoon? Not me!"

"And where does the storm come from, Stubb?" Starbuck shouted back. "Look! It comes from the east! It's on the same course that Ahab wants us to follow to find Moby Dick! And look at the hole in his whaleboat. Where is it? The place where Ahab himself stands! This voyage is cursed[55]!"

"What foolish things you think and say, Starbuck," said Stubb.

The chief mate went quiet for a moment. Then he said,

"We should turn the ship round and use this wind to blow us home to Nantucket."

At that moment the sky went black again and we were in complete darkness. Out of that darkness came a voice. It was followed by another crash of thunder.

The Typhoon

"Who's there?" said Starbuck.

"Old Thunder!" said Ahab. "Me!"

At first we could not see him. Then, with the help of a flash of lightning, we saw the captain walk to his place on the quarterdeck. He placed his ivory leg in the hole.

Starbuck suddenly remembered something. "The lightning rods!" he shouted. "Are they thrown overboard yet, men?"

On every high church tower you will always find a lightning rod, also called a lightning conductor. It is there to take the force of the lightning away from the church building and carry it safely to the ground below.

Ships have similar conductors—or rods—made from chains. They take the force of the lighting away from the ship and into the water. They are tied to a ship's mast, and must be very long. They must not touch the bottom of the ship when it's in the water.

"Don't worry about the rods, Starbuck," said Ahab. "We don't need them. Leave them where they are."

"Look up! Look up!" cried Starbuck. "Fire! Fire!"

We all looked up. The tops of the masts seemed to be covered in white flames.

"God save us all!" cried Stubb. He looked terrified.

The rest of us stood close together and stared silently up at the burning masts. We were too frightened to move. Then, suddenly, the flames all disappeared—and the masts were not damaged at all! The "flames" had been a strange light caused by a mixture of the air and the electricity in the storm.

"Do you still think I'm a fool with dark thoughts, Stubb?" asked Starbuck. "I heard *you* call to God to save us. This ship is cursed."

"No, no, you're wrong." said Stubb, with a little laugh. "I was asking God to look kindly on the fire. The flames were a sign of good luck. Those masts will soon be on a ship that's full of sperm oil. The oil will move up into the three masts and turn them into

The Typhoon

three candles. That's what I saw when I looked at them all lit up. Three candles!"

Before Starbuck could reply, he saw Stubb's face light up in the dark. The masts were burning again, twice as bright as before, casting ghostly shadows across the ship.

"Look!" Starbuck shouted. "Do you see now?"

"God save us all!" Stubb cried again.

All the crew moved closer to each other once more. We looked up at the masts.

Then I saw Fedallah go down on his knees beside Ahab.

"Yes, yes, men!" cried Ahab. "Look up at it carefully and understand what it means. That white flame lights the way to the white whale." He laughed loudly. "Give me those chains! Let me feel the lightning!"

He took the lightning rod in his left hand, then turned and put his foot on Fedallah's back. He pointed his right hand towards the masts and began to shout.

"Listen to me, fire! You've burned me before and this is your mark." He touched the white scar on the side of his face. "But you don't frighten me, oh no! You're a light that comes suddenly out of the darkness, but I'm the darkness jumping from that light! I'll put out your flames! It's *you* who will die!"

"The boat! The boat!" cried Starbuck. "Look at your boat, old man!"

The harpoon that Perth had made for Ahab was tied to its place in the whaleboat. We looked and saw the blade was covered in the same white fire as the masts.

Starbuck put his hand on Ahab's arm and held it tightly. "It's a sign, Ahab," he said. "God is against you, old man! This voyage is cursed. Do you understand? *Cursed!* It was cursed from the beginning, it will be cursed to the end. Let me put up new sails while we can. Let's turn the ship and sail for Nantucket. Perhaps then we can begin a better, safer voyage."

The Typhoon

When the crew heard Starbuck, we all cried out, "Yes! Yes!" and "Let's go home!" Then we ran towards the masts, ready to put up new sails.

Ahab immediately threw down the lightning rod and pushed through the crowd of men to his whaleboat. Then he took the flaming harpoon and waved it in front of our faces.

"Get back!" he shouted. "You signed on for this voyage to hunt the white whale, and so did I. And I'll work at it with every breath in my body, and every beat of my heart. Don't be afraid. Watch me blow this away."

Ahab lifted the harpoon to his mouth. Then, with one great breath, he blew out the flame. For a moment, we could not move. Then with terror in our eyes, we quickly went away from him. We could not believe what we had seen.

After two days, the typhoon became weaker and the storm slowly died away. Some hours after midnight on the third day, the last pieces of the old sails blew away. We put up three new sails and the *Pequod* finally began to sail steadily over the water. We were on course again. Starbuck went to Captain Ahab's cabin to tell him this. I was near the cabin and heard every word spoken.

Starbuck knocked on the cabin door and went in. Ahab was asleep on his bed. The captain's gun was next to him on a table.

"It's the gun he pointed at me," said Starbuck to himself quietly. He put out a hand and picked it up. "He was going to kill me," the chief mate carried on. "He doesn't care about anything except the white whale. He isn't worried about the dangers of lightning or typhoons. This crazy old man will risk his life and the lives of thirty or more men—and all for a whale! He won't listen to me, he won't listen to the captains of other ships. Is there a way to stop him? Make him a prisoner on the ship and take him home, perhaps? Only a fool would try to do it."

Ahab turned in his bed and Starbuck watched him.

"Is it wrong," the chief mate thought, "to murder a murderer?"

He lifted the gun slowly and pointed it at Ahab's head. "One push with my finger and you'll die, and I may live to see my wife and child again. But if I wake you, how deep down in the ocean may my body and the bodies of our crew lie, days or weeks from now? Great God, what shall I do?"

At that moment, words came from the mouth of the sleeping captain.

"Moby Dick! Moby Dick. I've got you at last!" he cried, twisting and turning in his bed.

Starbuck slowly lowered the gun and put it back where he had found it. Then he walked out of the cabin and back on to the deck.

14
The Rachel

We were sailing south-east towards the Equator. For days, everything was calm and quiet, and we saw no other ships. Then in the early hours of one morning, we sailed past some small islands of rocks. It was still dark.

Flask and the rest of us on the night watch were first to hear the strange noises. They were cries so wild and ghostly that we stood and listened to them without moving.

"What is it?" I asked at last.

"Mermaids[56]," explained one man.

"Mermaids?" I said.

"Mermaids lying on the rocks," said another sailor.

But the oldest man on the ship did not agree. "Those aren't mermaids you're hearing," he said. "Those ghostly sounds are the voices of newly-drowned sailors in the sea."

He lifted the gun slowly and pointed it at Ahab's head.

The Rachel

Ahab was still in his bed at this time. He did not hear about the noises until an hour later when he came on deck. Flask told him about them.

"They were wild, ghostly noises," said Flask. "That man says that they're the voices of drowned men."

Ahab laughed loudly. "Those rocky islands we passed are the homes of a great number of seals[57]" he explained. "Often the young seals get separated from their mothers. The sounds you heard were the mother seals searching for their lost children. They must have been swimming beside the ship."

Seals! This news did not make the crew any happier. Some sailors think that the sight of seals brings bad luck to a ship.

Later that morning, a man went from his bed to the mast. Perhaps he was only half awake and was beginning to fall asleep again. Nobody knows the truth. But we all heard his cry as he fell from the mast and into the sea.

We dropped the lifebuoy—a long, empty barrel with no ends—from the stern of the ship. The lifebuoy is supposed to keep a man afloat until he can be rescued by one of the boats. But this lifebuoy had been in the hot sun for too long. The wood had shrunk and seawater filled it in seconds, making it sink. We watched it follow our shipmate to the bottom of the sea.

The first *Pequod* sailor who had climbed the mast to look for Moby Dick in the whale's home waters, had drowned. Few of us thought about this then. It was the seals that had brought us this piece of bad luck, not Moby Dick—that's what we told each other.

Ahab ordered Starbuck to get the lost lifebuoy replaced. But no suitable wood could be found, and all the other barrels on the ship were too heavy.

Then Queequeg suggested using his coffin.

"A lifebuoy that's a coffin?" said Starbuck.

"Very strange," agreed Stubb.

The Rachel

But Flask disagreed. "It will be good enough," he said. Then he turned to some of the crew. "Fetch the coffin, and fetch the carpenter."

Minutes later, the carpenter stared at the coffin on the deck.

"Should I nail down the lid, sir?" he asked Starbuck.

"Yes, do that," said Starbuck.

"Should I make it watertight, sir?" said the carpenter.

"Yes!" shouted Starbuck. "Why are you asking all these questions? Go away! Do the work. Make a lifebuoy from the coffin!"

"Yes, yes, sir," said the carpenter. But he was not a happy man.

The next day we saw a large ship coming towards us. She was the *Rachel*, a large whaler. We were going along at a good speed before we saw her. But when she came closer, the wind suddenly went out of our sails.

"Bad news," said one of the men. "She's bringing bad news."

But before the *Rachel*'s captain could shout across to us, we heard Ahab's voice shouting to him over the water.

"Have you seen the white whale?"

"Yes, yesterday," came the reply. "Have you seen a whaleboat adrift?"

"No!" shouted Ahab, trying hard not to sound too excited about the news of Moby Dick. He was about to call for a boat to take him across to the other ship, but then he saw the *Rachel*'s captain climbing into his own boat.

We waited. A few minutes later, the other captain climbed aboard the *Pequod*. Ahab recognized him, but was too wild with excitement to talk about the days they had spent together in Nantucket. He only wanted to know about Moby Dick.

"Where was he?" asked Ahab, quickly. "Where? How? Not dead! Tell me he isn't dead!"

The Rachel

"No, he's not dead," said the other captain. And then he told his story.

"It was late yesterday afternoon," he said. "Three of our boats were chasing a group of whales when a white head and hump came up out of the water. We quickly lowered our fourth boat to chase him. It's our fastest boat, and we think its harpooner hit the white whale with his harpoon.

"He hit him?" Ahab asked, excitedly.

"That's what our man on the mast tells us, but he can't be sure," said the other captain. "He watched the fourth boat for as long as he could, but then it disappeared into the distance."

"What did you do?" asked Ahab.

"We weren't too worried," said the other man. "Whales often pull a whaleboat a long way away from the ship."

"Yes, they do," agreed Ahab.

"Also it was getting dark and the wind was getting stronger and we had to pick up our other three whaleboats and their men. They were going the opposite way from the fourth boat, and we had to turn the ship to get them. It was after midnight when we finally got them back safe aboard the *Rachel*."

"Too late to go after the fourth boat," said Ahab.

"Yes," said the other captain. "But we sailed after it as soon as it was daylight. We reached the place where our man on the mast had last seen it, but we found only empty sea. We lowered boats to search the area, but we found nothing."

"That's bad luck," said Ahab.

"We need your help to find it," said the other man. "With two of us looking we'll soon—" He stopped when he saw Ahab look away. "What is it? Listen, my own son is in that boat! He's only twelve years old and this is his first voyage. You have a son, Ahab, safe at home. You must understand how important it is for me to find mine."

"Captain Gardiner, I won't do it," said Ahab.

The Rachel

"What!" cried the other man.

"I can't take the time to search for your boat," said Ahab. "I'm sorry, but I have to go on. Goodbye and good luck."

"I won't leave your ship until you agree to help me," cried Captain Gardiner, angrily.

"Starbuck, give Captain Gardiner and his men three minutes to get off my ship!" said Ahab. "Then we sail!"

He turned and went back to his cabin. Captain Gardiner watched him go. For several moments he was too shocked to move. Then he climbed back down into his boat and returned to the *Rachel*.

Soon the *Pequod* and the *Rachel* went their separate ways. But for some hours we could see the other ship as it searched for her missing children. All her masts were full of men looking. But it was clear to us that they were having no luck.

It was a long time before I could get Captain Gardiner's shocked and unhappy face from my mind.

Now that Captain Ahab knew that Moby Dick was somewhere near, he could not rest and would not go to his cabin.

Whatever Ahab wanted, he sent for. He ate very little of the food that was brought to him, but watched the ocean day and night. His clothes that the rain made wet at night were dried by the sun the next day. His beard grew very long.

There was something in the old man's eyes that was frightening to see. It was a wild, strange look. He was a man who seemed close to madness.

Some of this strangeness seemed to be part of Fedallah, too. He stood without moving, hour after hour, watching the sea. And when he did move, he was like a silent shadow going about the ship. He was never very far from Ahab. And like our captain, he never seemed to sleep.

Ahab's cry of "Man[58] the mastheads!" was heard almost before

The Rachel

it was light. Every hour after that he was asking the look-outs, "What do you see? Can you see anything?"

Three days after we last saw the *Rachel*, Ahab himself went up the mast to be look-out. Perhaps he didn't trust his crew to tell him when they saw the white whale. He never said this, but we wondered about it.

"I'll have first sight of the white whale myself!" he said. "Yes, Ahab will have the gold coin!"

Ten minutes after Ahab reached the top of the mast, a large sea bird flew down around his head. The bird screamed and circled round Ahab for some minutes, but Ahab did not seem to notice it. He was busy looking towards the horizon.

"Your hat, your hat, sir!" cried one of the crew.

But the cry came too late. The bird had flown down and taken Ahab's hat from his head. With another loud scream, it flew away.

Day after day, the *Pequod* sailed on. One morning we saw another ship, the *Delight*. When she got closer, we could see a broken whaleboat along her side.

"Have you seen the white whale?" called Ahab.

"Look at this!" shouted the other captain. He pointed at the whaleboat. "He did it!"

"The white whale?"

"Yes!"

"Did you kill him?" Ahab wanted to know.

"Kill him? No! There's no harpoon that can do that," answered the other man, sadly.

"No harpoon!" shouted Ahab. He quickly picked up his harpoon and held it above his head. "Look at this! It's been touched by blood and by lightning. *This* will kill the white whale!"

"Then God help you, old man," replied the other captain. He pointed to a hammock[59] which two of his men were tying up. "I'm burying one man at sea now. Yesterday, he and four others were alive and well. Those four are in the sea already." Then he turned to his crew. "Are you ready?"

We watched from the *Pequod* as sailors from the other crew lifted the hammock on to a plank. Inside the hammock was the body of their dead shipmate. Then the captain said a short prayer[60] and the sailors sent the hammock down the plank into the sea.

"Set sail!" cried Captain Ahab quickly.

But the *Pequod* was not quick enough to escape the sound of the splash as the hammock hit the water. As we sailed away from the *Delight*, we heard a shout from the other ship.

"Look men!" One of their crew had seen our lifebuoy hanging at the back of the ship. "A coffin! They hurry away from our sad burial[61], but they carry their own coffins with them!"

15
Moby Dick!

It was a clear blue morning the next day. The sea and sky were the same color of blue, and the air was soft and warm. The sun was high in the sky and small birds circled round our masts as we sailed.

Ahab was walking up and down the deck, his eyes shining like two small fires as he stared out to sea. His beard was twisted and knotted and his face was burned a deep brown by the sun and wind. He looked over the side of the ship and watched his own shadow in the water. At first, the beautiful morning seemed to do nothing to improve his dark thoughts, whatever they were. But as the minutes went by his face softened. Then a tear slowly rolled down his cheek and fell into the ocean.

Starbuck was watching the old man. He saw how heavily Ahab leaned over the side of the ship. He moved and stood beside him.

Then the captain said a short prayer and the sailors sent the hammock down the plank.

Ahab turned. "Starbuck?" he said.

"Yes, sir," said Starbuck.

"Oh, Starbuck," said Ahab. "It's a soft, warm day, with a gentle wind. I struck my first whale on a day like this. I was a boy-harpooner, only eighteen years old. Forty years ago! I've chased whales for forty years, Starbuck. Forty years of storms, and all the terrible dangers of sailing. In all those years I've only been ashore for three of them. Sometimes I stop and think about my life. I think about the meals of dry bread I've been forced to eat when the poorest man on land has fresh fruit and bread on his table. I think about the time I've spent away from my pretty wife. On the day after we were married, I sailed for Cape Horn. I think about the way I've chased like a madman after whales, day after day. I've been a fool, Starbuck. Why do I do it?"

"Captain, you're being hard on yourself," said Starbuck.

"Am I, Starbuck?" answered Ahab. "How much richer or better am I after these forty years? Look at me! I've lost my leg in the hunt. Look at my scarred face. Look at my gray hair. I'm an old man. Old and tired. Stand closer to me, Starbuck. Let me look into a human eye. It's better than looking into the sea or sky. I see green land, and my warm comfortable home in your eye. I see my wife and child."

He put a hand on Starbuck's shoulder. "I won't let you risk *your* life, my friend," he went on. "Not when you have that far-away home that I can see in your eye. You and your men will stay aboard the *Pequod* when the chase for Moby Dick begins, Starbuck."

"Captain," said Starbuck. "Why should anyone chase that hated fish? He's a monster. Give up this chase for the white whale. Let's turn the ship around and head for home. Let's sail away from these deadly waters. How wonderful it will be to see old Nantucket again! They have beautiful blue days like this in Nantucket, I've seen them."

"It—it's true," said Ahab, slowly. "I've seen them too."

"Then let's sail for home!" said Starbuck. "My wife and son will be waiting there."

But Ahab turned away from the chief mate. He shook his head.

"No!" he cried. "No, we must go on!" Then he looked up at the sky. "Why can't I stop? What cruel, terrible thing inside me drives me on?"

Starbuck did not answer. Sadly, he turned and walked away.

Ahab went across the deck and looked over the other side of the ship. He looked down into the water and was surprised to see the reflection of another face looking up at him in it. It was Fedallah. He was looking over the same side, further along the deck.

———

That night, Ahab went to his usual place on the quarterdeck. Suddenly, he pushed his face forward and smelled the air.

"I can smell a whale," he said.

He was right. Soon all of the men on watch could smell that same smell. Ahab ordered a small change in direction and asked for the sails to be shortened. When it began to get light, he called,

"Man the masts! All crew on deck!"

Daggoo began beating the decks hard with a stick to wake up the rest of the crew. After a moment, men began to appear from below, some were only half-dressed.

"What do you see, look-outs?" shouted Ahab.

"Nothing, sir," came the reply.

"I'm coming up!" shouted Ahab.

He tied himself to some rope and the men pulled him up the main mast.

But before he had reached the top he shouted,

"There she blows! There she blows! Look! That hump of snow-white! It's Moby Dick!"

"There! There!" The other look-outs shouted at the same time.

We ran across the deck and climbed the rigging to look at the famous whale that we had been hunting for so long. Ahab at last reached the top of the mast, above the other look-outs. The whale was a mile or two ahead of us. Every roll of the sea showed us his white back.

"Didn't any of you see him earlier?" Ahab asked the look-outs.

"We saw him at almost the same moment you did, sir," replied Tashtego, who had been one of the look-outs.

"But not the *same* moment," said Ahab. "I saw him first. The gold coin is mine. There she blows, there she blows!" He shouted down to the deck. "Get three boats ready, Mr Starbuck, and remember to stay aboard ship with your crew. Now, bring me down to the deck. Faster, Starbuck, faster!"

Soon, all the whaleboats except Starbuck's were in the sea. We watched the three of them speeding through the water.

Ahab was in the first boat. As they got closer to the white whale, the ocean became smooth, like a carpet over the waves. Soon they could see the whole of Moby Dick's white hump moving through the water. Hundreds of white birds appeared suddenly and flew over the whale. A broken harpoon was sticking up from his hump, and the birds took turns to fly down and land on it.

The whale moved on. At first his head was still half-under the water, hiding his frightening jaws. Then, for a moment, almost the whole of him came slowly up out of the sea. He made a terrifying sound, then disappeared completely.

The three boats waited. "He'll be up again in an hour," said Ahab.

"The birds! The birds!" cried Tashtego.

The birds were flying towards Ahab's whaleboat. When they were near it, they flew over it in circles. Ahab looked over the

Moby Dick!

side of the boat and stared into the water. At first he saw only a white spot under the sea, but it grew bigger as it drew closer to the surface of the water. Suddenly, Ahab could see a long row of sharp teeth. It was Moby Dick's open mouth!

Ahab turned the boat with his steering oar and shouted to Fedallah to change places with him. Then he moved quickly to the front of the boat and took Perth's harpoon.

Suddenly, the whale's huge mouth came up out of the water. His teeth sank into the front of the boat so that he was lying on his back with his mouth high in the air. Then he began to shake the boat like a cat with a mouse in its jaws. The crew began to fall over each other to get to the other end of the boat. All except Fedallah, who sat silently watching with his arms crossed. The men in the other whaleboats were too shocked to move. They just floated and stared.

Ahab could not get a harpoon into Moby Dick and he quickly became very angry. He took the whale's jaws in his two hands and tried to open them, but it was impossible. After a minute or two, the jaws slipped through his fingers.

Moments later, the whale bit the boat into two pieces.

The two halves floated apart and Ahab and the crew jumped into the water. Moby Dick swam around them. He twisted and turned in the sea, pushing his great white head up and down in the water. For some unknown reason, the floating pieces from the broken boat seemed to make him angrier and angrier. He crashed his tail up and down in the water and made even greater waves.

Ahab suddenly found himself trapped in the center of this circle of very rough sea. Fedallah watched him from what was left of the stern of the boat. He did not seem worried. The rest of Ahab's boat crew were not able to help their captain. They were having difficulty staying afloat themselves. The crews of the other boats were afraid to come too near. They were afraid that the angry whale would rush in and kill the rest of the men in the water.

Moby Dick!

While all this was happening, we on the *Pequod* had moved closer to the wrecked boat. Now we were close enough to hear Ahab call out to us.

"Sail down on the whale!" he shouted. "Drive him away from me!"

Starbuck steered the ship forward, then moved her between Moby Dick and the men in the sea. As soon as the whale swam away, the other two boats rushed in to rescue their shipmates.

Ahab was pulled into Stubb's boat. There was very little strength left in his body. He fell into the bottom of the boat and lay there. But not for long. After a few minutes he sat up.

"My harpoon," he said. "Is it safe?"

"Yes, sir," replied Stubb. "I've got it here."

"Show me," said Ahab.

Stubb put the specially-made harpoon down in front of the captain.

"Are any of the men missing?" asked Ahab.

"No, sir," said Stubb. "All five are safe."

"That's good," said Ahab. He looked out at the sea. "I can still see Moby Dick. Look, there he is! Can you see his spout? Set sail! Get to the oars, men! Let's go after him!"

When men from one boat are rescued by those in another boat, the crew from the first boat will often help to row with the second. This happened now. But although Stubb's boat was now able to move faster through the water, it wasn't fast enough. Moby Dick was already swimming too far ahead to give them any hope of catching him.

"Back to the ship," ordered Ahab. "We'll follow him in the *Pequod*."

They rescued all that was left of Ahab's boat. This and the other two boats were then pulled up the sides of the *Pequod*, and the men climbed aboard. We were all glad to see them safe and well.

We set all the ship's sails and began to follow Moby Dick.

Time went on. Almost every hour a shout came from the look-outs.

"There's his spout!" they shouted. "There! There!"

And when the whale went under the sea again, the look-outs shouted once more.

"He's gone under, sir!"

Ahab would then look at the time. Exactly an hour later, he would say, "Do you see him?" Most often, the answer was "No, sir!"

Then Ahab would walk up and down the deck. Sometimes he stopped to look at the wreck of his whaleboat.

"It's a sad sight, Starbuck," he would say.

"Yes, sir," replied Starbuck.

The day was nearly finished. Soon it would be dark, but the look-out men stayed in their places.

"Can't see the spout now, sir!" cried one to Ahab. "It's too dark."

"All right!" Ahab shouted back. "Come down! Mr Stubb, send a new man to the masthead to be look-out until the morning."

Then the captain walked to the main mast and looked at the gold coin.

"Men," he said to the crew around him. "This gold is mine. I saw Moby Dick first, so I earned it. But the coin can stay here and the first man to see Moby Dick on the day that we kill him will get it. And if I am the one who sees him on the day I catch the great white whale, then I'll share ten times the value of that gold coin among you. Now, go to your beds."

16
Fedallah is Lost

As soon as it was light, the look-outs climbed the masts.

"Do you see him?" cried Ahab, who had stayed on deck all night.

"No, sir," came the reply. "We can't see anything."

"All hands on deck and set sail!" ordered Ahab. "He travels more quickly than I thought."

The men ran to put up more sails and the *Pequod* moved fast through the water.

"I can feel the speed of the ship in my feet and my legs!" said Stubb, laughing.

After some minutes, a shout came from the main masthead.

"There she blows! There she blows! Right ahead!"

"Yes, yes!" said Stubb, laughing. "I knew it. You can't escape, Moby Dick. The madman himself is after you. Ahab will get you!"

The rest of us were as excited as Stubb now. Whatever fears we might have had quickly disappeared at the thought of catching Moby Dick. After months of hunting the great whale across the oceans, and after the dangers of the day before, it was all we wanted. To catch and kill the monster.

"Where is he?" Ahab shouted to the look-outs. "Can you see him?"

"No, sir!" came the answer. "He's gone."

"Pull me up!" cried Ahab. "Let me look. Moby Dick doesn't just give one spout and then disappear."

We ran to the sides of the ship to look out as Ahab was pulled up the mast. Some men climbed on to the rigging to search the sea with their eyes. Where was the white whale? Then, suddenly, a huge cry went up from almost every man aboard.

"There! There he is!"

Fedallah is Lost

Moby Dick burst through the waves ahead of us. His whole body came up out of the water, and the spray around him shone like jewels in the sunlight. On he went, jumping out of the water and crashing down into it, again and again.

"Put down the boats!" cried Ahab.

The men jumped down from the rigging and ran to the boats. Ahab was brought down from his place on the mast and moved quickly across the deck.

"Mr Starbuck, stay aboard the ship," he said. "Keep away from the boats, but keep near them."

The three whaleboats and their men were quickly put down into the water. Almost immediately, Moby Dick turned and began to rush towards them. Ahab's boat was between the other two. He stood up and shouted orders to his crew.

"Sail towards the middle of his head!" he told them.

It was an old whaler's trick. The whale's eyes are on either side of his head, so that he cannot see what's coming straight at him. A hunter will try to get as near to the whale as he can before the great fish sees him.

But Moby Dick turned and opened his jaws as he saw the boats coming. Then his great tail went up—and crashed down among the three boats. The harpooners all threw their weapons into his side, but he twisted and turned so many times that the three lines became caught around him and slowly the three boats were all pulled in towards him. Ahab let out more line to try to shake free from the whale, but it was no good. After a moment, he took a knife and cut the line.

At that moment, the white whale rushed at the other two boats. Their twisted lines pulled them together so fast they crashed into each other before Stubb or Flask could stop them. Every man was thrown into the water.

Immediately, Moby Dick dove down into the sea, leaving the wrecks of the two boats and their crews floating in the water above him. Stubb was shouting for help. Flask held on to a piece

Fedallah is Lost

of his broken boat and tried to pull his legs up away from any passing sharks.

Ahab's boat was not damaged, but suddenly Moby Dick came up under it and lifted it out of the water and into the air! He turned it over and sent it crashing down again, into the sea. Ahab and his men screamed with terror as they fell into the water.

Then Moby Dick swam away, pulling the broken lines behind him.

Starbuck and the rest of us aboard the *Pequod* had watched it all happen. Now we steered towards the broken boats to rescue the men before they drowned or were taken by sharks. We put a boat down into the sea and picked up floating men, oars, wooden planks and whatever else we could catch. Several of the men were hurt, but not badly. We brought them all back up on deck.

We found Ahab holding on to his boat's broken half. When at last he came aboard, every man's eyes were on him. He was holding on to Starbuck's shoulder. His ivory leg had been broken off, leaving only one sharp piece fixed to him. Stubb came forward quickly.

"Are you hurt, Captain?" he said.

The carpenter was near him. "I'll make you another leg, sir," he said to Ahab.

"I'm all right," Ahab told them. "Moby Dick has broken my leg, but he won't stop me." He shouted up to the look-outs, "Can you see him?"

"Yes, sir! To starboard!" the look-out shouted, pointing.

"Put on more sails again, Mr Starbuck," said Ahab. "Let's go after him!"

"First let me help you to your cabin, Captain," said Starbuck.

"I don't need your help," said Ahab. "Give me that broken spear, I can use that to walk with. Where's Fedallah?"

We all looked round but could not see him.

"Search the ship!" ordered Ahab. "Find him!"

For the next twenty minutes we looked everywhere, but we could not find Fedallah.

Fedallah is Lost

"He must have been caught in your twisted line, Captain," said Stubb. "I thought I saw him go under when— "

"My line? My line?" shouted Ahab.

"Yes, sir," said Stubb.

"So Fedallah's gone. Lost," said Ahab. "It's what he told me—that he would die first. My harpoon's gone, too. Did you see it, Stubb? I sank it into the white whale's side with my own hand! Ha!" Then he looked up at the masts and shouted, "Lookouts, watch for Moby Dick! Don't lose him! Crew, put on more sails, collect the oars, sharpen more harpoons. We'll catch that monster yet!"

"Dear God, no!" cried Starbuck. "You'll never catch him, old man. Please, no more of this madness. For two days we've chased him. Twice you've gone after him and seen our boats broken into pieces. You've lost your leg again, taken by the same whale as before. Now Fedallah's gone, too. How many more warnings do you need? Must we chase this monster until every man is drowned? Are we all to go to the bottom of the sea in this cursed ship? We must stop now!"

"Ahab is Ahab, and he can't change," said Ahab, quietly. "I can't stop until it's finished, Starbuck."

Then he turned to the crew. "Men, listen to me! You see an old man, cut down to one leg, held up by a spear. I may look like a broken man, but I'm not! Twice Moby Dick has escaped from us. For two days he's floated. Tomorrow will be the third day. Drowning things often rise to the surface twice before sinking forever. Moby Dick will rise a third time, but only to spout for the *last* time. "Do you feel brave, men?"

"As brave as fire!" cried Stubb.

We followed Moby Dick until it was dark. Then, all through the night came the sound of hammers as we repaired our boats and made fresh weapons for the next day's hunt. The carpenter worked through the night as well. He was busy making Ahab another leg.

17

The Second Hearse

The next morning it was fine again. There was a clear blue sky and a steady wind. The look-out on the fore-masthead was soon joined by men climbing on the rigging. They were all hoping to be the first to see Moby Dick.

"Do you see him?" called Ahab.

"No, sir!" was the answer.

"Nothing?"

"Nothing, sir."

"Then we've gone past him," said Ahab. "He's chasing *me* now! We must have gone past him in the night. He will be slower with all those harpoons sticking in him. Turn the ship around! Come down all of you, except the look-outs."

A few minutes later, we were sailing hard against the wind.

"Against the wind and towards the open jaws of a monster," Starbuck said to himself. "God help us!"

"Get ready to pull me up the mast," cried Ahab. "We should meet Moby Dick soon."

"Yes, yes, sir," said Starbuck.

And once more Ahab went to the top of the mast.

A whole hour went by.

We waited.

At last Ahab called, "There she blows!"

At the same time, three shouts came from the three mastheads,

"There she blows!"

"So, I meet you for the third time, Moby Dick!" cried Ahab. "You men on deck, get the boats ready. Steer into the wind! He's too far away to put the boats down yet, Mr Starbuck. He travels fast."

The Second Hearse

"Should we bring you down from the mast, sir?" asked Starbuck.

"Not yet, Mr Starbuck," cried Ahab. "Let me have one more good look round at the sea. There's time for that. I first saw the ocean from the beach at Nantucket, and it's the same today. The ocean never changes."

He was silent for a moment, then he said, "Now steer away from the wind! The whale is going that way. Goodbye, old mast. We grow old together, you and I. Keep a good eye on the whale for me. All right, Mr Starbuck, bring me down."

Ahab was lowered to the deck. The boats were now ready to be put down into the sea.

"Starbuck!" called Ahab.

"Yes, sir?" answered Starbuck.

"I begin this voyage for the third time," said Ahab.

"Yes, sir, if you must," said Starbuck.

"Some ships sail and never return, Starbuck," said Ahab.

"That's true, sir," said Starbuck. "Sad but true."

"Shake hands with me, my old friend," said Ahab.

"Don't go, Captain!" said Starbuck and his hand, shaking Ahab's, was wet with tears.

"I *must* go. Lower the boats!" ordered Ahab. "Crew, get ready to sail!"

The boats went slowly down into the water.

"Sharks! Sharks!" came a cry from a low cabin window. "Captain, come back!"

But Ahab did not hear the voice of warning over the sound of his own shouting, and the crews rowed away from the ship. Within moments, all three boats were surrounded by sharks. They came up from the dark waters under the ship and immediately began trying to bite the oars each time they went into the sea.

It is not unusual for sharks to follow whaleboats. They seem to know the times when they might be provided with fresh food.

The Second Hearse

But these were the first sharks we had seen from the *Pequod* since we first saw Moby Dick.

The sharks circled all three boats for a time, then they all went after Ahab's boat.

They had not gone far when the white whale disappeared under the water. All the crews stopped rowing and waited silently. Suddenly the water around them began to make waves. A sound came from under them—and a moment later Moby Dick burst up out of the sea! There were harpoons and spears in his back, and he was pulling broken lines behind him. Seconds later, he crashed back down into the water.

"Forward!" shouted Ahab.

The boats moved quickly forward to attack. The whale came rushing towards them, his tail making huge, dangerous waves around them. He pushed Stubb's and Flask's boats apart, sending the spears and harpoons into the water and making holes in the sides of the boats. Ahab's boat was not damaged.

Daggoo and Queequeg tried to fill the holes as the whale turned and swam away from them. Now they could see the other side of the great fish.

Suddenly they saw Fedallah! His half-torn body lay caught under the twisted lines, he was tied to the whale's side. His dead eyes stared out at Ahab. Ahab saw him and his harpoon dropped from his shaking hand.

"I can see you, Fedallah!" he cried. And at that moment he remembered Fedallah's words.

"I will die before you and show you the way ... you won't die until you have seen two hearses on the sea ... the first hearse will not be made by human hands ..."

"Is Moby Dick the hearse you promised?" cried Ahab. "He's not made by human hands, that's certain! But where's the second hearse?" He turned to Flask and Stubb. "Go back to the ship, men!

Fedallah's half-torn body lay caught under the twisted lines.

The Second Hearse

Those boats are useless now. Repair them if you can, then return to me." He watched the damaged boats move away, towards the *Pequod*. "Now, where's the whale? Has he gone down again?"

But Moby Dick was swimming away from him and had almost passed the *Pequod*.

"Ahab!" shouted Starbuck from the ship. "It's not too late to stop the hunt! Look how Moby Dick swims away from you. It is you who looks for him, not he who looks for you. Let him go, sir!"

Some minutes later, the wind turned Ahab's boat around. Soon he was close enough to the *Pequod* to see Starbuck's face looking down at him.

"Turn the ship round and follow me!" Ahab ordered. "Not too fast."

He looked up and saw Tashtego, Queequeg and Daggoo climbing the three mastheads. The two boats with holes in them had been pulled up on to the side of the ship. Their oarsmen were busy repairing them. Stubb and Flask were on the deck, working among new spears and harpoons. As Ahab saw all this, he felt a deep sadness in his heart.

The sharks were still around Ahab's boat. They swam along beside it, biting the oars of the rowers.

"Pull, men! Pull!" shouted Ahab. At the same time he wondered who the sharks were planning to eat, Moby Dick, or himself?"

"But our oars are getting smaller and smaller with every bite," cried the rowers, as they looked over the sides of the boat at the sharks.

"They'll last long enough," said Ahab. "Pull! We're near Moby Dick now!"

Minutes later, they were beside the great white whale. But Moby Dick swam on without stopping or turning. Ahab swore loudly at his hated enemy and threw his harpoon into the whale's body.

The Second Hearse

Immediately Moby Dick rolled over in the water and crashed against the whaleboat. Ahab held on to the sides, but three of the rowers were immediately thrown into the sea. Two managed to climb back aboard, but the third was left swimming in the water.

"Hold the line!" shouted Ahab. "Pull the boat up to Moby Dick!"

At first the wet rope slipped through the men's hands, but at last they held it. But as soon as the rope was stretched tight, it broke and Moby Dick swam away free.

"After him!" screamed Ahab. "Don't let him get away!"

The whale heard the whaleboat rushing through the water after him and turned round. He saw Ahab and the rowers. Then he saw the *Pequod* coming just behind them. Suddenly he began to swim fast towards it.

"Look at the whale!" cried the rowers. "He's going towards the ship!"

Tashtego, on the top of the main mast, saw the creature swimming towards them and shouted a warning. Starbuck and Stubb saw him at the same moment.

"God help us!" cried Starbuck.

Every man on the ship stopped working and ran to the sides. They watched in terror as that great white head came closer and closer to the ship, but there was nothing they could do.

The whale hit the ship and every part of it shook violently. Men were thrown on to the deck as a great hole was forced into the starboard side of the *Pequod*. Immediately, there was the sound of water rushing in.

"My ship!" screamed Ahab. "It's the second hearse!"

Then Moby Dick dove and swam under the *Pequod*. He came up again near Ahab's boat. For a time he lay quietly in the water, watching the *Pequod* sinking.

Ahab watched her, too. "My wonderful ship!" he cried. "Must you die without me? This is the worst thing that can happen to a captain, not to be with his ship when it sinks!'" Then Ahab took a new harpoon and went to the front of the whaleboat. "I'm coming for you, you hated whale!" he shouted at Moby Dick. "I'll kill you, even if it takes the last breath in my body!"

He stood tall in the boat and threw the harpoon into the whale. Moby Dick flew forward, and the line went away fast from the boat. It caught on an oar and Ahab tried to get it free. He *did* get it free, but as it flew it caught him round his neck and pulled him out of the boat. He had disappeared under the water before his crew realized what had happened. They never saw their captain again.

The rest of the rope went out of the boat and Moby Dick swam away.

The whaleboat stopped moving in the water. The crew stood still for a moment, then they turned.

"Dear God!" cried one man. "Where's the *Pequod*?"

Only the masts were above the sea now. The harpooners and look-outs had climbed to the top of them, but they could not save themselves. Moments later the broken whaleboat was sucked into the whirlpool[62] created by the sinking ship. Soon the boat and its rowers were all sucked under as the ship finally went down into the ocean.

Sea birds flew over the waves for a while, then the sea rolled on as it always has for many thousands of years.

But one man did not drown. Who was it? *It was me, Ishmael.*

After Fedallah was killed, Ahab ordered me to take his place in the whaleboat. *I* was that third man who was thrown out of the boat on that last day. *I* was the one left swimming in the water when Moby Dick hit the side of the boat. I was some distance away from the *Pequod* when she sank. But I was pulled gently towards the place where the ship went down, turning in circles and not able to stop myself.

Then suddenly, something came up out of the sea. It was Queequeg's coffin! It had broken free from the sinking ship as she

The Second Hearse

went down. Now it floated on the surface of the water. I swam across and pulled myself on top of it.

For a day and a night I floated on a gentle sea. Sharks swam past me, sea birds flew over me, but I was safe aboard the coffin.

The *Rachel* eventually found me. Her captain and crew were still searching for their missing whaleboat and their missing children. Instead, they found me.

Another missing orphan[63].

Points for Understanding

1

1 Why did Ismael think that it was time for him to go to sea again?
2 He decided to go to sea as an ordinary sailor. What did we learn about Ishmael from this decision?
3 He planned to go to Nantucket. How might that help him fulfill his dream?
4 Ismael had to share a bed in the inn. What was unusual about his companion?
5 The sailors on a whaling ship had different jobs. What were they?

2

1 The preacher spoke about Jonah. Why did he tell this story?
2 What interesting things did Queequeg tell Ishmael about himself?
3 Which of these three men: Bildad, Peleg or Ahab was the captain of the *Pequod*?
4 What was Ishmael told about this man?

3

1 "A troublemaker" and "crazy". Do you agree with these opinions about Elijah? Give reasons for your answer.
2 The *Pequod* was being prepared for her long voyage. How?
3 What do you think the warning was that Elijah wanted to give Ishmael?

4

1 There were three mates on the *Pequod*. Give their names.
2 In this chapter, Ishmael saw his captain for the first time. Do you think he now felt more hopeful or more worried about the voyage? Give reasons for your answer.
3 Why did Ahab ask his crew these questions?
4 He was offering a prize. What was it and what did a man have to do to win it?
5 The crew knew a good deal about Moby Dick. List the known facts.

5

1 Why were these five crew members called ghosts?
2 Where had Ishmael seen them before?
3 Why was Ishmael shaking with cold and fear at the end of this chapter?

6

1 How much success did the whale-hunters have in this chapter? Explain what happened to them.

7

1 What was unusual about the whale's sight?
2 When a whale had been caught and killed, what did the crew have to do?
3 Gabriel said that he was a prophet. What did he say about the future?
4 What information about Moby Dick did the captain of the *Jeroboam* give Ahab?
5 What was Tashtego's special job and how did it nearly kill him?
6 How was he saved?

8

1 Something happened that allowed the *Pequod's* boats to catch the German one. What was it?
2 The crew of the *Pequod* caught a whale, but they had to let it go. Why?
3 Captain Ahab had planned the next part of his journey carefully. Where exactly was he going?
4 Queequeg managed to harpoon a whale, but that put his boat in danger. How?
5 Is it lucky for whalemen to come across a school of whales? Give the reason for your answer.

9

1 How did Stubb manage to trick the captain of the French ship, the *Rosebud*?
2 Stubb had a plan. Show how successful it was.
3 The dry whale smelt awful and then, suddenly, a sweet smell came from it. Explain how that happened.

10

1 Pip had experiences that made him go crazy. Who should be blamed for that?
2 Ahab went on board the *Samuel Enderby*. What made him do that?
3 What did he find out from the ship's captain?
4 The two captains had a disagreement about Moby Dick. Which one did you think was right, and why?

11

1 Ishmael overheard a conversation between Ahab and Starbuck. Say what they were talking about and what the conversation told you about them.
2 Summarize Queequeg's behavior after he gets sick.
3 He then made a decision. What was it?

12

1 Captain Ahab wanted his new harpoon to be made in a different way. What made it different from usual harpoons?
2 The *Pequod* met the *Bachelor*. In what ways was that a lucky ship? How did the *Bachelor's* luck help the *Pequod*?
3 Ahab and Fedallah spoke about Ahab's death. What was Ahab told? Did he believe it? What else did he believe?

13

1 Starbuck thought that the voyage was cursed. Why did he think that?
2 Stubb, Ahab and Starbuck all thought that the fires meant different things. Explain their ideas.
3 Starbuck thought that Ahab was a crazy old man. Do you agree or not? Give your reasons.
4 Starbuck had the chance to kill Ahab, but he did not. What do you feel about that?

14

1 What caused the strange noises that the men heard?
2 Why was Queequeg's coffin used as a lifebuoy?
3 Why did Captain Ahab refuse to help Captain Gardiner?
4 The *Delight* had news of the white whale. What was it?

15

1 Captain Ahab had many regrets about his life. What were they?
2 Why did Ahab shout, "The gold coin is mine!"
3 How was Ahab saved from the white whale?
4 Ahab made two promises. What were they?

16

1 The crew's feelings had changed, How?
2 Although Moby Dick was not human, he seemed to have a plan. What was it?
3 Ahab had a plan too. What was it?

17

1 What was Ahab's plan after he saw Moby Dick for the third time?
2 How did the sharks make the hunt more difficult?
3 What had happened to Fedallah?
4 Moby Dick had his revenge on Ahab. How?
5 How did Ahab die?
6 What happened to the rest of the men?

Glossary

1. **merchant ship** (page 4)
   a ship that carries goods rather than soldiers and weapons.
2. **voyage** (page 4)
   a long trip, especially by boat or into space.
3. **crew** (page 4)
   the people who work on a ship, aircraft, etc.
4. **cannibal** (page 4)
   someone who eats human flesh.
5. **manuscript** (page 4)
   a writer's original pages of a book, article, or document before it is published.
6. **fuel** (page 5)
   a substance such as oil, gas, coal, or wood that produces heat or power when it is burned.
7. **harpooner** (page 5)
   There are many tools and *weapons* in this book. A *weapon* is an object that can be used to hurt people or damage property. A *harpoon* is a weapon consisting of a blade on a pole attached to a rope, used for hunting whales and big fish. Someone who uses a *harpoon* for hunting is called a *harpooner*. An *ax* is a tool used for cutting down trees and cutting up large pieces of wood, consisting of a long wooden handle and a heavy metal blade. A *tomahawk* is a small ax used as a weapon in the past by Native Americans. A *spear* is a long weapon like a stick with one sharp end.
8. **fierce** (page 5)
   very angry or ready to attack.
9. **irritable** (page 7)
   likely to be easily annoyed or impatient.
10. **magnificent** (page 7)
    very impressive and beautiful, good, or skillful.
11. **coffin** (page 8)
    Here, it is the last name of the landlord but is usually a long box in which a dead person is buried.
12. **embalmed** – *to embalm* (page 8)
    an *embalmed* dead body, or part of a dead body, has been preserved using chemicals.

13 **tattooed** – *to tattoo* (page 9)
   A *tattoo* is a permanent picture that is drawn on a part of your body by putting ink into your skin with a needle. If you *tattoo* someone, you draw a *tattoo* on someone's body.
14 **pipe** (page 9)
   an object used for smoking tobacco, consisting of a tube with a small bowl at the end.
15 **shaved** – *to shave* (page 11)
   to make a part of your body smooth by cutting off the hair.
16 **mate** (page 12)
   a junior officer in a navy. On a ship, the *chief mate* is the highest in authority. The *second mate* is the next highest in authority, and the *third mate* is the third highest in authority.
17 **rank** (page 12)
   someone's official position in the military, police force, fire department, etc., or someone's status in society compared to the status of other people.
18 **aboard** (page 14)
   in or on a ship, train, or airplane.
19 **she** (page 15)
   used mainly in literary language for referring to a nation, a ship, or a car, when it has already been mentioned or when it is obvious which one you are referring to.
20 **stained** – *to stain* (page 15)
   to leave a mark on something accidentally. If something is *weather-stained*, marks have been left on it by the weather.
21 **shrugged** – *to shrug* (page 16)
   to move your shoulders up and let them drop to show that you do not know something or do not care.
22 **will do** – *something will do* (page 16)
   used for saying that something is enough or can be used for a particular purpose.
23 **profit** (page 16)
   money that you make by selling something or from your business, especially the money that remains after you have paid all your business costs.
24 **shipmate** (page 18)
   a sailor who works together with another sailor on the same ship.
25 **scarred** – *to scar* (page 18)
   to leave a permanent mark on someone's skin as the result of an injury or illness.

26 **ahoy!** (page 20)
   used by sailors for calling to people on other ships.
27 **coward** (page 21)
   someone who is not brave enough to fight or do something difficult or dangerous that they should do.
28 **puzzling** (page 22)
   confusing or difficult to understand or solve.
29 **anxious** (page 23)
   worried because you think something bad might happen.
30 **took it in turns** – *to take turns* (page 23)
   if people *take it in turns* to do something, each of them does their share of it, one after the other.
31 **hammer** (page 24)
   a tool used for hitting things or forcing nails into wood, consisting of a handle and a heavy metal top with one flat side.
32 **revenge** (page 25)
   something that you do to hurt or punish someone because they have hurt you or someone else.
33 **barrel** (page 25)
   a round wooden, metal, or plastic container with a flat top and bottom, used for storing liquids.
34 **rowing** – *to row* (page 27)
   to move a boat through water using long poles with flat ends called *oars*.
35 **persuaded** – *to persuade* (page 28)
   to make someone agree to do something by giving them reasons why they should do it.
36 **bubbling** – *to bubble* (page 31)
   A *bubble* is a ball of air or gas in a liquid. If liquid bubbles, *bubbles* form and move in it.
37 **squid** (page 32)
   a sea animal like an octopus but with ten arms instead of eight.
38 **ivory** (page 35)
   something that is ivory is a yellowish-white color.
39 **starboard** (page 36)
   the right side of a ship, as seen by someone who is looking toward the front. The left side is called *port*.
40 **prophet** (page 36)
   according to some religions, a man sent by God to lead people and teach them their religious beliefs.

41 **beg** – *to beg* (page 39)
   to ask for something in a way that shows you are not proud.
42 **cargo** (page 41)
   things that are being sent by ship, airplane, train, or truck.
43 **pirate** (page 42)
   someone who attacks ships while they are sailing in order to steal things from them.
44 **school** (page 43)
   a large group of whales. *Cows* are female whales, and *calves* are young whales.
45 **tangled** (page 51)
   if something is *tangled*, its parts are twisted around each other in a messy way.
46 **damn** (page 51)
   an impolite expression used when you are annoyed about something.
47 **the Equator** (page 53)
   an imaginary line that goes around the Earth and divides it into the northern and southern hemispheres.
48 **accurate** (page 60)
   correct or true in every detail.
49 **anvil** (page 61)
   a metal block on which a blacksmith shapes metal objects with a hammer.
50 **rod** (page 62)
   a long thin bar or stick made of metal, plastic, or wood.
51 **razor** (page 62)
   a small tool used for shaving – removing hair from your skin.
52 **barb** (page 62)
   a short curved point on something such as a fish hook that makes things difficult to remove.
53 **hearse** (page 65)
   a large car used for carrying a dead person in a coffin.
54 **hangman** (page 65)
   someone whose job is to kill people by hanging them.
55 **cursed** (page 67)
   if you *curse* someone, you use magic powers to make bad things happen to them. If someone or something is *cursed*, they are affected in a negative way by a magic curse.

56 **mermaid** (page 70)
an imaginary sea creature that has the upper body of a woman and a fish's tail.
57 **seal** (page 72)
a large ocean animal that eats fish and lives mainly in cold parts of the world.
58 **man** – *to man something* (page 75)
to provide a place, machine, or system with the people needed to operate it.
59 **hammock** (page 76)
a bed consisting of a long piece of cloth or net tied at each end to posts or trees.
60 **prayer** (page 77)
the words that someone says when they are speaking to God.
61 **burial** (page 77)
A *burial* is usually the process of putting a dead body into a grave in the ground at a funeral. In *Moby Dick* the *burial* is a *burial at sea*, in which the dead person's body is dropped into the sea.
62 **whirlpool** (page 95)
a strong movement in water in which the water moves around in a circle and pulls things under.
63 **orphan** (page 96)
a child whose parents have died.

Dictionary extracts adapted from the Macmillan English Dictionary © Bloomsbury Publishing PLC 2002 and © A & C Black Publishers Ltd 2005.

Further Study Questions

Plot

1 Order the events in the story.
   - [ ] A man warns Ishmael against joining the crew of the *Pequod*
   - [ ] Ahab sees Moby Dick for the first time
   - [1] Fedallah is pulled from his whaling boat by Moby Dick
   - [ ] Ishmael decides to go to sea
   - [ ] Moby Dick attacks the Pequod
   - [ ] Queeqeg's coffin floats to the surface of the sea
   - [ ] Ishmael sees a group of mysterious men join the ship
   - [ ] The *Pequod* meets a ship (the *Rachel*) that has lost a boat during the hunt of the white whale
   - [ ] Ishmael meets Queeqeg
   - [ ] The *Pequod* is struck by an electrical storm

2 Think about the importance of each event. How does it help develop the story?

   Example: *Ishmael meets Queeqeg. Ishmael is the narrator and the reader's first introduction to the strange world of whaling.*

3 A prophet is a person who makes prophecies (statements about the future). Prophecies play an important part in the plot of *Moby Dick*. Which characters makes the prophecies below? Which ones came true?
   1 *"Any man who sails on that ship will never return."* (p20)
   2 *"Beware of the white whale! ... Think of your whaleboats, holed and sunk! Think about your men, lost or drowned!"* (p37)
   3 *"You won't die until you have seen two hearses on the sea ...the first hearse will not be made by human hands. The second will be made from a tree that was grown in America"*. (p 65)
   4 *"I shall die first and show you the way."* (p65)
   5 *"I shall not die before I kill Moby Dick!"* (p65)
   6 *"And only rope can kill you old man."* (p 65)

   How does each prophecy add to the mystery and suspense of the plot?

4 The *Pequod* meets other whaling ships on its voyage. Each ship has a story to tell. Consider the importance of each ship and what it tells us about a) the business of whaling b) the hunt for Moby Dick.

The *Albatross*:	a ship that has been at sea for a long time, the sailors are tired and the ship looks in bad condition.
The *Jeroboam*:	the crew have a fever, they have lost one of their men to Moby Dick. Gabriel, one of the sailors on board, shouts a warning to Ahab.
The *Jungfrau*:	a German boat. Its crew need oil for their lamps. Ahab gives them oil before both ships go after the same whale.
The *Rose-bud*:	a French ship carrying two sick whales. Stubb tricks the captain and takes one of the sick whales for its ambergris.
The *Samuel Enderby*:	an English ship. The captain lost his arm hunting Moby Dick.
The *Bachelor*:	an American ship on its way home after a good voyage. It has been very lucky and has caught hundreds of whales.
The *Rachel*:	its crew have lost a whaleboat that was chasing Moby Dick. The captain's son is on board. Ahab refuses to help look for the boat.
The *Delight*:	they have lost five men because of Moby Dick. They are giving the fifth man a burial at sea as the *Pequod* sails by.

Essay question

Prepare to write an answer to this question.

> Moby Dick is a sea adventure. Discuss how prophecies, superstition (a belief in the power of magic and luck) and stories told by other whalers add to the mystery and suspense of the plot.

Characters

1. It can be argued that there are three main characters in the novel, Ahab, Moby Dick and Ishmael. Who do you think is the most interesting? Why?

Ahab

2. Do the adjectives below give an accurate description of Ahab? Why/why not? Can you think of any other adjectives to describe him?
   - mad
   - superstitious
   - charismatic (having a strong personality that attracts and influences people)
   - obsessed (unable to stop thinking about something or someone)

3. Think about these questions and give examples from the story to support your answers.
   - Is Ahab a good captain? Does he look after his boat and crew? Does he think about the needs of other boats at sea?
   - Is he a good leader of men? How does he persuade the whalers to help him hunt down Moby Dick? Think about how he uses the sailors' fears and superstitions.
   - Does Ahab have to die? What would he have done with the rest of his life if he had succeeded in killing Moby Dick?
   - Why is killing Moby Dick so important to Ahab?

Moby Dick

4. It can be argued that Moby Dick is more than just a whale. Think about these questions.
   - What do we know about the great white whale?
   - Who gives us the information?
   - Is the whale trying to kill Ahab?
   - What does the whale represent ?

Ishmael

5. Ishmael is the only survivor of the adventure. Look at the questions below and think about his character.
   - What do we know about Ishmael and his past life? Why does he decide to go whaling?

- Ishmael tells the story of Moby Dick. Can we trust his descriptions of events and people? Why/why not?
- Imagine Ahab is the survivor, not Ishmael. In what way would the story be different?

Essay question

> Discuss the character of Ahab. He is stubborn, selfish, revengeful and destructive, but there are times when we feel pity for him. Explore both sides of the man, his obsession and his humanity.

Themes

The whaling industry

1. *Moby Dick* includes detailed descriptions of the whaling industry. Think about what we learn in the novel about:
   - sperm whales, sperm oil, ambergris
   - the process of hunting a whale
   - the crew of a whaling ship and their various tasks

2. Discuss what you think it would be like to work on board a whaling ship in the 19th century.

Revenge

3. Look at this conversation between Ahab and Starbuck (p 25) and discuss the questions below.

Ahab: "It was Moby Dick that took my leg and I'll chase him round the Cape of Good Hope and Cape Horn, and across the world before I let him get away!"

Starbuck: "I'm here to catch whales, not to satisfy the revenge of my captain. Whaling is my business, but how many barrels of oil will your revenge get us? To be angry with an animal is crazy."

- Do you think it is understakable for Ahab to want revenge?
- What price does Ahab pay for his revenge?
- What does Ahab's obsession with Moby Dick tell us about the nature of revenge?

Superstition

4 The *Pequod* comes across the dead body of a giant squid (p32). Read the two statements below. Which is based on fact and which is based on superstition?
- *"The dead body of a great squid," said Starbuck. "Very few whaling ships see one and return home to tell anyone about it."*
- *"When you see a squid," he told me as he pointed his harpoon toward the sea, "you'll soon sea a sperm whale."*

5 Consider how these other 'signs' appear to the sailors, the captain and Ishmael.
- The typhoon (pp 66–69)
- The sound of seals calling to their young (pp 70–72)

6 As the ship gets close to Moby Dick, superstitions seem to become more important to Ishmael and the others sailors than fact. Discuss why this happens and what it tells us about the sailors and their feelings about the hunt.

Essay question

Choose one of the following questions and write a full answer.

As well as an amazing story about an amazing adventure, *Moby Dick* is also a record of life aboard a whaling ship in the mid 19th century. What do we learn about the whaling industry from the novel?

Discuss how Ishmael gradually introduces us to the world of Captain Ahab and the great white whale. How are other people's descriptions and stories used to introduce the characters before they make a direct appearance?

Discuss the great white whale. What does Moby Dick represent? In what ways does the whale represent different things to different people? Think about the crew of the *Pequod*, and the captains and crews of other ships that they meet on their voyage.

For help with these questions, visit www.macmillanenglish.com/readers

Macmillan Education
4 Crinan Street
London N1 9XW
A division of Springer Nature Limited
Companies and representatives throughout the world

ISBN 978–0–2300–2687–2

This version of *Moby Dick* by Herman Melville was retold by John Escott for Macmillan Readers

First published 2008
Text © Springer Nature Limited 2008
Design and illustration © Springer Nature Limited 2008
This version first published 2008

All rights reserved; no part of this publication may be
reproduced, stored in a retrieval system, transmitted in any
form, or by any means, electronic, mechanical, photocopying,
recording, or otherwise, without the prior written permission of
the publishers.

Illustrated by Fausto Bianchi and Martin Sanders
Cover by Getty Images/Stone

Whilst every effort has been made to trace owners of copyright material in this book, there may have been some cases when the publishers have been unable to contact the owners. We should be grateful to hear from anyone who recognises copyright material and who is unacknowledged. We shall be pleased to make the necessary amendments in future editions of the book.

Printed and bound in Uruguay